Best wishes from

Tony Jenkins
9/1/22

The author was born in South Wales and originally worked as a mining surveyor before joining the RAF to begin training as a navigator. After completing his service, he began working for an international company in sales and marketing and was appointed managing director of a subsidiary company. He decided to become self-employed as a management consultant and then retired to play tennis and write.

To my wife, Margaret, who persuaded me to give up building walls and write novels instead. Her advice and help in proofreading were invaluable.

Tony Jenkins

TOO SLOW TO DIE

AUSTIN MACAULEY PUBLISHERS™

LONDON • CAMBRIDGE • NEW YORK • SHARJAH

A CIP catalogue record for this title is available from the British Library.

ISBN 9781528932349 (Paperback)
ISBN 9781528932356 (Hardback)
ISBN 9781528967013 (ePub e-book)

www.austinmacauley.com

First Published (2020)
Austin Macauley Publishers Ltd
25 Canada Square
Canary Wharf
London
E14 5LQ

The publishing team at Austin Macauley could not have been more helpful and their support made my work much easier.

Chapter 1
Extradition

Commissar Dalca read the request from the Hungarians for the extradition of one of their subjects. Their man was named Renko Veres and he was accused of multiple murders, corruption and theft, and was believed to have fled to Romania. Dalca was wondering why the man would want to come to his country, until he read that Veres was a Tigani, or Roma. Dalca spent much of his time reading reports of crimes committed by these people and he knew that the man could well be hiding in any one of the hundreds of Tigani communities throughout his country. The Hungarians would have to provide him with information of the likely location, before he would consider allocating any of his limited resources to chasing after one of their renegades, even if he was a mass murderer.

Five weeks after tossing the Hungarian request into his heavily loaded 'pending' file, he was surprised to receive another communication from the Hungarians. They now wanted to cancel their extradition request because they had learned from a reliable source that the man, Veres, had been crucified and killed. His body had then been burned at the village of Budestin in Călăraşi County. The small village was near the Transylvanian mountains with steep valleys and extensive forest areas. The roads leading to it were very poor and it was the last place he would have chosen to investigate a crime. Its only advantage was the variety of wild animals living in the surrounding forest, which would be a good source of food and appealed to his hunter's instincts.

Although pleased that he would not have to allocate men to find the fugitive, Dalca was furious that the Hungarians seemed to know far more about what was happening in his country than he did himself. Both countries had not long broken away from the communist yolk and were jealous of their newfound independence. He was not surprised that the Tigani had killed the man, but he was not going to let them get away with murdering a foreign national and he intended to teach them a lesson. He called in his assistant, Bojin, and ordered him to bring him details of Tigani men serving in their militia ranks. He hoped he would be able to find a suitable candidate to send to the northeast corner of the country to investigate whether the claim by the Hungarians was true. He knew that only another Tigani was likely to be accepted by the people at Budestin. If his man could gain their confidence, it should be possible for him to find evidence or witnesses to the crime.

The man he chose for the investigation was named Gunari. He had served ten years in the militia and been born in the western area of the country and would not be known in Budestin. At his briefing, he was told that he should claim to have been discharged from the army for insubordination and that he was now trying to settle back in civilian life. Gunari was thirty years old, unmarried and was a tall man with curly black hair and deep-set brown eyes. He had been trained to obey all orders, but looked forward to working independently instead, and spending time amongst the carefree Tigani people he had grown up with. Although he had served and volunteered for special training in various sections of the militia and excelled at most, he was still a private. Recently, he had decided that his failure to gain promotion could only be because he had been born a Tigani.

Private Gunari was given a month's pay in advance and told that any expenses he incurred during the operation would be refunded on his return to the barracks. It was also intimated that if he did a good job on his mission, it could lead to a promotion. To save time, he was driven to an isolated spot, roughly thirty miles from Budestin and told to make his way on foot for the remainder of the journey. By passing through other Tigani communities first, he would then be able to support his story about wandering north and arriving in Budestin on his travels.

Gunari was told that at the end of a month, or sooner if he found the information required by the commissar, he should leave Budestin and make his way south to the nearby town of Bacău. From there he should telephone his base orderly room and transport would be sent to collect him. He would then make his report in person to Commissar Dalca. After spending the nights in two different villages on his journey north through Călăraşi County, it was the middle of the afternoon on the fourth day when he reached the Tigani settlement at Budestin. The village was near a large pine forest, which was usually a good source of food for the Tiganis. He could see wispy trails of grey smoke drifting slowly into the blue sky from the homes and cooking fires.

After seeing a group of people gathered around a large central fire, he made his way towards them and saw the mix of expressions on the faces turned towards him. None of them showed any hostility as he approached, but he knew they were suspicious of strangers. Once he had introduced himself, he could see their tension ease as they recognised from his dress and speech that he was one of them. A place was quickly made for him near the fire and he was offered food from the large cooking pot suspended over the flames and an old woman assured him that a bed would be found for him. As he was eating his food, a large man came and sat beside him, before telling him that he was named Tigo and he was the leader of the people at Budestin. Taller than Gunari and with long, black hair tied into ringlets and a spikey beard, he was broad shouldered and very sure of himself. As well as the long knife at his waist, he carried a new rifle, which he carefully placed on the ground beside him.

Chapter 2
Investigation

Six weeks had passed since Private Gunari set off on his journey to Budestin and so far, he had made no contact with his superiors. Commissar Dalca and his assistant wondered whether Gunari had deserted, been harmed, or was being held captive by the locals. He would certainly not have disobeyed his orders to contact them from Bacău. Impatient and determined to get answers, Dalca ordered a twelve-man squad of armed soldiers to travel to Budestin and search for Gunari and any evidence that the man, Veres, had been crucified and killed. The soldier in charge was Sergeant Dinescu, a hardliner and long-service veteran. After taking a full day to make the drive north from their base outside Bucharest, the men arrived at Budestin as the early morning meal was being prepared by the women. The group around the cooking pots looked up in alarm as they watched armed soldiers approach and then surround them. They stopped their preparations and stared defiantly at the unwelcome visitors.

The sergeant cradled his rifle across his chest and looking down at the seated women, asked who was their leader. After receiving no response from the sullen group, he repeated his question and eventually an elderly woman got slowly to her feet and stepped forward to stand before him. She held two hands, palm up in front of her chest and gave her answer to his question.

"Our leader is Tigo, sir, but he has gone away."

"And when did this Tigo go away, old woman?"

"Perhaps, five days, or even six days, sir."

As they were speaking, twelve-year-old Fonso climbed a nearby tree to get a better view of the big soldier standing close to his grandmother. He could tell from her voice that she was frightened of the man carrying the big gun.

"Tell me, old woman, did this Tigo travel alone when he left, or did he go off with someone else, a stranger perhaps?"

"I was asleep in my bed when he left, sir, and I cannot say."

Irritated by the old woman's unhelpful answers, Dinescu moved closer and took hold of her arm. With his face near to hers, he spoke again.

"We have a report from some Hungarian visitors to your village that you people murdered another Hungarian called Renko Veres. What do you know about that, old woman?"

Wanting to protect his grandmother, Fonso placed a good-sized stone in his sling and took aim at the soldier. The stone flew past the sergeant's head and struck a soldier behind him on the forehead, splitting the skin. The soldier raised his hand to the wound and feeling the sticky blood running down his face, he anticipated some sort of attack. Looking around the area, he saw movement in a tree at the forest edge and reacted instinctively. Raising his rifle, he fired into the centre of the shaking leaves. His gun was set on automatic fire and as the bullets tore through the branches, a shower of leaves and wood fragments exploded into the air and then the body of young Fonso tumbled down to the ground below. With a roar, the watching women and some old men suddenly turned on the soldiers. The startled young men were forced to defend themselves with their rifle butts as they were attacked with cooking pots, logs and knives. The fracas lasted only three minutes before the well-armed and trained soldiers succeeded in subduing their attackers.

There were several bodies on the ground and amongst them were three of the soldiers. Although two were soon sitting up and nursing bruised heads, the third lay motionless, with the wooden handle of a cooking knife protruding from his chest. As a colleague used a field dressing to try to stem the blood flow, those soldiers who were still standing, kept their rifles trained on the now subdued and frightened Tigani. The sudden noise had roused the men from their beds and they began to gather alongside their women and shout abuse at the armed soldiers, who looked apprehensively towards their sergeant. As he took stock of the growing numbers, Dinescu could see that he and his men were now outnumbered by more than ten to one. He was also concerned about the injured soldier and knew that the man needed urgent hospital attention. Looking at the enraged faces surrounding them, he knew that he could not expect any cooperation from the villagers. Ordering his men to pick up their wounded colleague and walk slowly back to their truck, he kept his gun trained on the angry mob around them.

There was a hospital at Bacău and his wounded soldier was given immediate attention, but after the three-hour-long drive over poor roads, the man had lost a great deal of blood and he died before the doctors could take him to the operating theatre. Dinescu telephoned his superiors with details of the attack on the soldiers and the absence of their fellow soldier, Gunari, at the village. The information was immediately forwarded to Commissar Dalca. Already hostile to the Tigani, the death of one of his soldiers and the attack on his men caused him to smash his fist on his desk in anger. After thinking again about the reported crucifixion, followed by the possible killing of his own man, Gunari, the commissar decided that those responsible must be punished and he ordered drastic action.

A week later, a much larger detachment of soldiers surrounded the Tigani community in Budestin as dawn was breaking and quietly took up their positions. Men, women and children were suddenly roused from their sleep by armed soldiers smashing in their doors with rifle butts. They were then driven from their homes by belligerent soldiers, who wanted revenge for the earlier death of their colleague. The old woman who had previously spoken to Sergeant Dinescu on the previous visit, recognised him and came rushing at him with a long-bladed knife raised over her head to strike at him. Without hesitation, the sergeant raised his gun and shot her dead. He later discovered that she was the mother of the leader, Tigo, and guessed that she was probably responsible for stabbing to death one of his men on their last visit. Those who resisted, or tried to remove valuables from their homes were savagely beaten and driven away. The soldiers then set fire to the wooden houses and soon all that remained of the Tigani community in Budestin was a devastated area of black smoking ruins and charred belongings.

The Romanian villagers who lived nearby watched as the soldiers systematically destroyed house after house and drove everyone who lived there into the surrounding forest, but refused to help their Tigani neighbours. They considered that the Tigani people had provoked the brutal reprisal by their hostile reaction to the government soldiers. Although a thorough search of all the houses had been carried out, the soldiers found no trace of their missing colleague, Gunari, or the mysterious leader of the Tigani community named Tigo.

The Tigani village at Budestin no longer existed and when he received the report of the confrontation and clearance, Commissar Dalca considered that whatever had happened to the fugitive, Veres, and his own man, Gunari, the law had been upheld and there was nothing further to be done. After writing details of the two visits by the militia in his files, Dalca sent a brief report to the Hungarian authorities, assuring them that the people responsible for murdering their man, Veres, had been punished and the matter should now be considered closed. Unfortunately for him and for many others, both in Romania and Hungary, it was only just the beginning.

Chapter 3
Construction

Two figures stood on the edge of a giant crater carved into the ground and looked down at the men and machines busily working below to tear bauxite ore from the earth. It was now six months since the Hun-Al mine had begun operating on family-owned ground, with Demeter Pusztai as the chief executive and Jack Randil as a member of the board. The two men had become firm friends after surviving an attack at night by thugs near the Eiffel Tower in Paris. This was followed by an attempt by two armed local Romas to kill Demeter, which had been foiled by Jack. The would-be assassins had dressed as policemen and intended to shoot Demeter at his isolated Pusztai mansion at Dunakeszi, some twenty kilometres north of Budapest in Hungary. Jack had anticipated the attack and from his sniper position on the first floor, had wounded both armed men, who were then handed over to the real local police.

A giant bauxite mine in Australia was able to extract ore very efficiently, but it then had to be shipped thousands of miles to supply the European market. To meet local demand, a new opencast mine had been established three miles from the Pusztai house, where the ore was found in a two-metre thick seam. It was then carried in enormous lorries to the refinery on the shore of the Danube, which made use of water from the Danube and oil from Romania in the processing. It took two and a half tonnes of ore to make a tonne of alumina and two tonnes of alumina was needed to make one tonne of aluminium. Although demand for the ore was high as European industries expanded their operations after the fall of the Iron Curtain between the West and Russia, the two men knew that they must do everything possible to reduce their production costs.

Big savings would be made if an industrial rail line could be built to carry larger quantities of bulk ore from the mine to the Pusztai refinery near the River Danube. From the riverside dock, the aluminium ingots would then be shipped to customers throughout Europe. Unfortunately, the direct route from the mine to the refinery passed straight through the middle of a Roma village.

Although the village was on Pusztai land, it had grown to accommodate more than two hundred people since it began with just half a dozen caravans some fifty years previously. The next Hun-Al board meeting would have to decide whether the rail link should be built, as well as its route. Demeter Pusztai was chairman of the company and owned the land, but the mining operation was financed by the Hungarian government, which had appointed most of the board members. Jack Randil had been nominated by Demeter, because of his business experience, European contacts and foreign language fluency. The men were also close friends and Jack was the only non-Hungarian appointed. The board meeting was scheduled to take place in Budapest, the following morning.

There was Roma blood in Demeter's veins and in spite of this, his family had suffered imprisonment and deaths in the long battle as to who should inherit the Pusztai land and businesses. Demeter's life was twice saved by Jack Randil, who now looked after Paul, the young son of Demeter's sister, Arianne, who was killed on a French farm by two Roma assassins. Her husband, Pat Mears, who had previously been married to Jack's sister Mary, was murdered at the same time.

"I know you are not happy about building the rail line through the village, Demeter, but surely the Roma people will just have to move on to a new site, which has always been their way of life. If it eases your conscience, you could even offer them alternative land to set up their new homes. I am sure the government will insist that you reduce your costs and since they control most of the votes, their view will dominate."

"I know you are right Jack, but these people have always been exploited, exterminated or ignored and considered as second-class citizens. During the war, 28,000 Hungarian Roma were taken to Auschwitz concentration camp by the Germans and very few survived. They have become nomads because they are frequently forced to move by the locals. They really want to make permanent homes so that they can get work and their children get an education. For them, the Dunakeszi site is their permanent home and if they are now forced to move, who could blame them for doing everything they can to stay."

"I know how you feel about these people, Demeter, but during the past few years you have had nothing but trouble from the Roma, so you should be well prepared. You know that the rail line is essential and is certainly going to be built as quickly and as cheaply as possible, with or without your agreement."

The two men left the Pusztai mansion early the following morning, for the drive to Budapest and their route took them past the steep hill alongside the Danube where Demeter's car had been forced off the road by men hired by Renko Veres to kill him. He shivered as he remembered the cold waters of the Danube closing over his head and appreciated just how lucky he had been to survive. He loved his country, but from the time he had attained his teens, his life had always been in danger.

Commissar Radics had been appointed to the Hun-Al board by the government as security and manpower director and Dorika Biro had been chosen because she was an experienced geologist. She had worked for a number of foreign mining companies and was determined to build her own country's mining industry. The remaining four directors were also government appointments and covered transport, engineering, administration and procurement. Jack was the commercial and export director. Although the land and deposits were legally his, the government was financing the project and in spite of his position as chairman, Demeter would be forced to follow Hungarian government policies.

Extraction figures for the bauxite ore were on target and the refined ingots exported via the River Danube were already bringing much needed foreign exchange earnings. World demand was strong and Hungary should be able to gain a small share of a big market. It was in competition with the giant companies in Australia and India, but by operating on slim profit margins and supplying the surrounding countries, it was slowly building its turnover. The Government's top priority was to make more profit and it was Radics who proposed that an industrial rail line be built, linking the mine with the refinery. He had already located both the rails and a small steam engine at a defunct arms factory used by their German allies during the Second World War. He explained that coal was readily available to fuel it and was cheaper than the imported diesel oil currently being used by the giant lorries moving the ore.

Demeter suggested curving the rail track around the Roma settlement, but Radics insisted that he had insufficient track to do this and it would also take too much time and money. Put to the vote there was a clear majority to build directly through the settlement. Demeter proposed compensating those Roma whose homes were bulldozed, but this was also rejected. Radics suggested that Demeter should contact his 'non-paying Roma tenants' and tell them about the impending rail construction and offer them any alternative land he had in mind.

During their return car journey, Jack advised Demeter to avoid going into the Roma settlement to tell the people about the rail construction. He urged him instead to invite their leader Boldo to meet him at the Pusztai mansion and then explain about the rail line and offer of a new site. The construction work and house clearance would badly disrupt the Roma community and once completed, the railway would dominate the area and operate for eighteen hours every day. By meeting Boldo alone, he would avoid possible violence against him as the owner of the mine and land, when the Roma learned that they would have to leave their homes.

After receiving the meeting invitation from Demeter, Boldo arrived at the Pusztai mansion in a very old Dacia car, which belched out clouds of black smoke from its battered exhaust pipe. He had not come alone to the meeting, but was accompanied by a tall, bearded-Roma who was introduced as a family member from Romania, who spoke no Hungarian. The man had alert but deep-set eyes and although he neither spoke, nor smiled, his eyes moved constantly around the room and Jack could tell that both he and Demeter were being assessed. Although the man was some inches shorter than him, Jack sensed that the Roma would nevertheless be a dangerous opponent.

Boldo showed no surprise when told about the rail line construction and wasted no time in making his response.

"Many of our people have found work in your big mine and that is a good thing. They have heard that the special earth you dig up must be taken in big lorries to be mixed with water from the river. There has already been much talk about a rail line to replace the lorries. We know our village stands in your way and Roma people have no rights and must move, unless you build around our village. We have been happy on your land for many years and have made it our home, which is why we ask that you do not force us to leave."

"I am genuinely sorry, Boldo, but the company has to build a rail line and unfortunately, there is not enough rail track to build around your people. You know my land well and I would like you to choose where you want to move and build new homes."

"Many of my people do not like the dust and the noise after the quiet and good air which we knew before the mine opened. Some will leave and others will not give up where they were born. We are poor people and if you force us to move to the north of your land, we will be further away from Dunakeszi town where we have our regular customers, as well as the work in the mine. Since the government wants us to move, will they also give us money to help us to build new homes?"

"The government has very little money, Boldo, and what there is they need to build up our industries. We can use our lorries to help your people to move and to take your men to the mine. I have little money myself and I am working to repair this house after the new government gave it back to me, but I will help as much as I can."

Boldo asked when the rail construction would begin. Demeter explained that the rail track had first to be delivered to the dock near the refinery and work would then start to build towards the mine, using completed rail line to move materials. His guess was that work would begin within a month.

"Must I speak with you if there are any troubles?"

"I will not be involved with building the railway, but you can come to me whenever you need my help and I will speak with Larjos Farkas, who will be the man in charge of the railway."

The meeting ended and Boldo shook hands with Demeter and Jack. His companion had already turned away and begun walking to the car. The two Roma men drove away leaving behind them a cloud of oily black smoke floating in the morning air. Demeter was surprised that news of the possible rail-link had already been leaked, but Jack knew how quick workers were to piece together chance comments and guess possible outcomes.

"Do you think we can build this line and move the Roma without trouble, Jack?"

"I doubt it and whatever happens, I feel sure that our silent bearded Romanian visitor will be involved. I was watching the body language and it was clear that Boldo was very nervous of his friend. If there is going to be trouble, it will probably happen when the track building gets near their village and they have to start clearing out their houses. I am flying back to Liverpool in two days to look after my business, but keep in touch and if you need me, I can be here within hours. Although I have only been here a week, I am already missing my family, just as you must be missing Theresa. When are you two getting together again?"

"The house still needs a lot of work, but we are going to meet for a few days in Budapest and then I am hoping to bring her to see the Pusztai mansion and try to describe how it was and how it will be again when I have finished the restoration. The stables were magnificent, but I can't afford to rebuild them, or buy horses. I know I am lucky that the arsonists didn't burn down the house instead."

His fiancée, Theresa was studying marketing at Durham University and was the daughter of Jack's sister Mary, who had divorced her father, Pat Mears. Her father had later married Arianne Pusztai and both were murdered in their French farmhouse. Demeter had met Theresa during a visit to Liverpool to see his sister. The two had recently become engaged and planned to marry after she had taken her degree in marketing at Durham University. They both hoped that they would be able to live at Dunakeszi and work together to restore the mansion to its old splendour.

Chapter 4
Competition

After surviving a horrific car crash on the M5 Motorway, Jack Randil lay in a coma for two weeks before waking to find that his memory and senses had become far sharper. Somehow, the blows to his head had allowed his conscious and more powerful subconscious mind to form a link. Using his extra sensory abilities and his natural commercial flair, he had built a small family business into a major company in Liverpool. As well as owning Randil Building Services, he had become a city councillor and chaired the Planning Committee, as well as the Liverpool Trades Council. He also had a seat on the board of a local engineering company.

When Demeter's sister, Arianne, and her husband were murdered on a French farm, Jack and Demeter had followed their killer, Renko Veres, to Romania to bring him back for justice. Instead, they had been forced to watch as the man was crucified and then killed. The communist regime in Hungary had confiscated the Pusztai lands and properties, but when freed from Russian dominance, the new government had returned them and was now financing the bauxite mine.

After agreeing to work with Demeter on the mine, Jack had drastically reduced his business commitments by resigning from Liverpool Council and giving up his seat on the engineering company board. His company Randil Building Services had a competent management structure and by chairing the Liverpool Trades Council with its strong European connections, he planned to make use of his time and contacts to develop aluminium exports from the Hun-Al mine. He was also learning to speak Hungarian.

Arriving at his home late on Friday evening, it was almost like another honeymoon being greeted by his wife, Judy, when he came through the front door and they wrapped their arms around each other. He had spent the past week in Hungary and with the children asleep in their beds, the young couple were able to show how much each had missed the other. Jack was pleased to hear how Arianne's four-year-old son, Paul, was getting along with his own four-year-old boy, Leighton, so that they were like brothers. Paul was entitled to a half-share in the Pusztai lands and businesses, as well as full ownership of the French farmhouse and land. He was also a half-brother to Theresa.

As he drifted off to sleep with Judy in his arms, Jack wondered if one day Demeter would ask Paul to move to Hungary so that he could learn the Hungarian language and customs and eventually become involved in the family business. Until then Jack wanted to give Paul a loving family background and a good education to prepare him, whatever his future might be.

Jack was at his desk before 7 am on Monday morning to work through the neat piles of papers set out by his staff, so that he could catch up on company activities. There were reports that two of their security guards had been attacked as they checked buildings where Randil provided security cover. There had been no attacks previously and now two had taken place within a week. Jack sent for his brother-in-law, Greg Ridd, who was in charge of his security operations.

"Hi Jack and welcome back. I can guess what you want to talk about."

Greg explained that two of his men, who worked alone had been attacked and beaten by a group of men who had lain in wait for them at each of the premises. Both men were ex-military and were trained in unarmed combat, but wooden pick handles were used on them and the attacks were well planned and sudden. Both men had been taken to hospital when they were able to use their mobile phones and summon help. The company had very good relations with Liverpool police and they could rely on their cooperation and information.

"So Greg, there was no damage to property, or to customer's staff and the attack was entirely directed at our men. Do you think it was intended to be severe enough to make them worried about doing their job alone in unoccupied premises at night?"

"That is just how I am seeing it, Jack. We look after a lot of properties and have a big reputation in the city. I'm checking if there are any new companies in the area, which want to expand their security business at our expense. I also checked with our best customers to ask if anyone had offered similar cover at lower prices and none of them had been approached."

"Good thinking, Greg. Whoever is behind this is moving carefully. Our men carry batons and phones as well as press-button remotes for use in emergencies, so they must have been taken by surprise. Perhaps, we should have them wear helmets with visors to save them from dangerous head injuries."

"Good idea Jack, and why not send our men out in pairs so that they can protect each other."

"Yes, do that Greg. I believe we are providing a service to the city and since we know the police don't have the staff to help us, I wonder if we can make use of their equipment. Perhaps, we could get hold of pepper sprays for all our men. I know they are illegal, but if they use them only when attacked, the attackers are not going to complain and admit they were involved. Perhaps, we can capture a couple of these men, whoever they are, and try to find out who controls them."

"Great Jack, but until we get the sprays, can I fix them up with helmets and double-up on patrols by taking on extra men through our big friend, Joe Devine."

"Yes, and give the big man my regards. We must arrange a reunion of the Town Hall group. I can't believe that it was only last year that we were trapped in those old tunnels, or how lucky we were to survive those fanatics."

The business was doing well and after his meeting with Greg, he wandered around the building to chat with staff and maintain his personal links. There were sixty people working in the office and warehouse, but his mind kept returning to the team of security men facing an unknown attacker. He was concerned that his men had been injured and decided he must get more involved. He called in on Greg to make arrangements to join one of the security men on his rounds that night.

Greg was not happy to have his boss putting himself at risk, but was unable to make Jack change his mind, especially when Jack guessed that Greg himself had already arranged to accompany one of his men. After telling Judy that he wanted to find out how his security men performed in the evening, he and Greg met up with two security men covering the Fazakerley area of industrial units. Jack paired up with an ex-marine called Graham as he began his regular journey, but he suggested varying the call sequence to avoid arriving at the usual time. If there were intruders waiting for them, they could be caught off guard when their victim did not arrive at his usual time. Graham drove the van and Jack sat out of sight at the back.

After making four regular checks without problems, they let themselves in to a large technical laboratory owned by a multi-national group. Jack let Graham lead and followed behind with his hand on a metal baton he had bought in Singapore. As they approached a right-hand-turn in a corridor, Jack's sharp senses picked up the smell of body odour. He tapped Graham on the shoulder and waved him back so that they could go forward together. Jack took left and Graham right. There were men waiting around the corner for them, but they did not expect two security men in helmets to appear and strike them with batons. Two men were immediately knocked to the ground, but two more were waiting behind, who charged at their intended victims.

One unsuspecting security man had been an easy target, but two helmeted security men wielding batons was something else. It was also payback time for the cowardly attacks on their colleagues. The exchange was short, but ended with four attackers unconscious and laid out on the ground. Jack and Graham taped their hands and feet together and Jack called his police contact to come and collect four intruders, who had burgled the building and attacked them. Once the intruders were helpless, Jack went through their pockets to check identities for future use, but none of the men carried any papers. The police van arrived within twenty minutes and collected the four, but they remained stubbornly silent.

Jack stayed with Graham until he had completed his visits and then left to return home to his wife, who was not happy about his arrival in the early morning. He was satisfied that the change of routine and preparation had been successful, but was concerned that all four assailants had remained totally silent, before and after the police arrested them. Most felons would either have protested their innocence, or screamed for a solicitor as soon as the police arrested them.

Next morning, he learned that Greg and his companion had completed their night checks without incident, but his friend had already heard about Jack's clash with intruders from Graham. As they were speaking, the telephone rang and Jack spoke to his squash partner and ex-best man, Detective Inspector Peter Kilshaw.

"Hi Jack. I see you wasted no time after getting back from Hungary to attack more of our local citizens. Still none of them were shot this time. You must be losing your touch."

"And good morning to you too, Peter. Always willing to lend a helping hand to our local constabulary. Have they said anything yet?"

"Not a word Jack, and I expect you already know that they carried no identification, which makes me think they are foreign and decided to go into business in Liverpool. I remember the last foreign tourists you and Greg attacked in that car park and I hope that there is not going to be another run of killings. Can you drop in and let me know what you know and think is going on? My superintendent is already worried that you are starting another crime wave."

"Tell him he has nothing to worry about and as usual, I will take care of everything. Be there within the hour."

Chapter 5
Retribution

Commissar Dalca had cleverly managed to improve his position as the old communist regime crumbled, and the new 'free' government took power. Like many other officials, he had previously worked for the communists, but his change of loyalties and past behaviour had not proved a hindrance. He now held an important position, which gave him more advantages than ever and he welcomed democracy as long as it mainly benefitted him. It was Friday and as he finished his working week before driving home, he took an admiring look around his comfortable office with views over Bucharest. He enjoyed the warm glow of satisfaction in having yet again fallen on his feet. His newly purchased large house was near a forest and over the weekend he would again be taking his gun to enjoy himself hunting. His wife had been complaining that a brown bear was raiding her garden and waste bins and he would enjoy killing the animal to prevent any further rampages.

His dinner was delicious and he complimented his wife on her cooking before they settled down for the evening to watch foreign programmes on their new television. Dalca thought how lucky they were and how they could now look forward to enjoying a comfortable future together after the turmoil suffered by their country. Unfortunately, his beautiful dream would soon be shattered.

Outside his home at the edge of the forest, a hooded figure wearing bulky dark clothing, shaded his eyes against the setting sun, after spending another day watching the house. Satisfied that his target would remain indoors for the night, he opened his sleeping bag and wrapped himself up to settle down under the trees and sleep. He was looking forward to his meeting with Commissar Dalca the next morning, and having studied his movements over the past week, he had already picked out a number of suitable spots where he could attack him.

After enjoying a good breakfast, Dalca put on his expensive, new hunting clothes and strapped a leather cartridge belt around his ample waist, then kissed his wife and left the house. It was a bright and sunny morning with a blue almost cloudless sky as he walked off to look for the persistent bear targeting his home. It was an ideal day for hunting and as there were no other houses nearby, Dalca had become accustomed to having the forest to himself. There were many other wild animals in the forest, including wolves, deer, chamois, lynx, wild boar, foxes and pheasants. It was a hunter's paradise and not more than a twenty-minute walk from his house.

After waking at dawn to begin watching the Dalca house, a figure in crumpled clothes and with a mask covering his face, carefully followed Dalca as he walked towards the dense part of the extensive forested area. Unaware of the stalker behind, Dalca began looking for bear droppings and claw marks on the tree bark to locate the animal's usual route to his house. After walking backwards and forwards through the trees for over an hour, he finally found scattered droppings and chewed bone fragments, which showed that he had located likely bear tracks at last. He loaded his gun, switched on the safety catch and began to move more carefully through the rough grass as he looked around for his prey.

The masked figure made his way carefully around Dalca and then threw a large stone into a thickly wooded patch to Dalca's right to draw his attention. Hearing the noise in the bushes, the commissar switched off the safety catch and raised his rifle as he stood still. He waited, hoping that the bear would come out of the trees and give him a clear shot. Suddenly, he heard a gunshot from behind him and felt a hammer blow to his right leg. Crying out with the pain, he dropped his rifle and clutched at the wound, as blood streamed down his trouser leg. He did not see the figure approaching him until he was thrown forward on his face and felt his arms being bound behind him with some sort of tape. Although his face was pressed down into the coarse grass, he managed to scream at his attacker.

"Who are you and what are you doing. Do you know who I am?"

He received no answer and instead, tape was wound across his eyes so that he could no longer see what was happening around him. Then Dalca felt his clothes being cut from his body and shivered at the sudden chill of the forest air on his skin. He was horrified to realise that he was naked, apart from his hunting boots and socks. He cried out again.

"Stop this. What do you think you are doing?"

Again, there was no answer and he felt a heavy blow to the side of his head, which left him dazed. Then his legs were tied together so that he was completely helpless with a rope wound around his ankles. The other end of the rope was flung over a thick tree branch and although Dalca was quite a heavy man, his captor had no trouble hauling him into the air until he hung from the branch, with his head only eighteen inches above the grass below. His captor spoke to him.

"Why did you send soldiers to Budestin?"

"The Hungarians wrote to me that someone called Renko had been crucified and killed and I sent a man to investigate, but he failed to contact me."

"How did the Hungarians know what happened to Renko?"

"They told me that two Hungarians were at Budestin when Renko was killed."

"What was the name of the soldier-leader who killed the old woman?"

"It was Sergeant Major Dinescu, but the old woman tried to stab him with a big knife and he had to defend himself."

Nodding his head after getting the information he wanted, the man then wound tape around Dalca's mouth to make sure that he could no longer speak. With Dalca swinging slowly from the branch, the man then used his knife to make small cuts in the victim's forehead and chest so that blood began to drip down to the grass below. Satisfied that any passing animals would smell the blood and investigate before beginning to enjoy a meal from Dalca, the man walked away. He did not want Dalca to bleed out before feeling himself eaten by forest animals. He had killed the marauding bear the previous day, and moved its body deep into the forest. It would have made short work of a helpless Dalca and the man was determined that instead, his victim would die slowly and painfully for his crimes.

Left alone with his body slowly swinging on the rope end, Dalca strained his ears to identify the sounds around him. Why had the man done this to him? He had never shown any concern for those he had sent to their death, or prison and finally he began to experience what a helpless victim feels. Eventually, he heard a rustling noise and sensed that something was standing near him. A cold nose brushed his face as an animal sniffed at him and Dalca frantically twisted his body to try to get away from the inquisitive beast. Hearing sounds of quick movement, he hoped that he had frightened it away from him. Minutes passed and then he felt a burning pain in his face as something bit and tore away part of his cheek. Unable to cry out, or defend himself, he desperately tried to swing his body away from the animal and once more, the movement drove it away. Tense and desperate and listening for any movement, he hoped that it would now leave him alone, until he felt his nose gripped with sharp teeth and torn away from his face.

The horror of his predicament and his inability to see, or cry out was putting unbearable pressure on his sanity. This combined with the aching pain from his wounded leg and the increasing agony from the bites to his flesh, tipped his mind into an escape from reality.

Walking back to collect his sleeping bag and other equipment, the man saw Madame Dalca busily working in her vegetable garden, but he had no quarrel with the woman and carried on walking back to the bus stop for his return journey to Bucharest.

When her husband did not return for his lunch, his wife became worried that he had been injured by the bear and telephoned his office. Saturday afternoon was a time when many were off duty, but a search team of six men was finally assembled by late afternoon. By the time darkness prevented further searching, the team had failed to find any sign of Dalca, although they did find the carcass of an old brown bear, which had been shot recently. They made their way back to the Dalca house and reassured the distraught wife that they would resume the search the next morning.

A group of twenty men arrived early the next morning and Dalca was finally found, suspended from the tree branch. Although unconscious, the man was still alive, but only just. He was carried back to his home and then rushed to hospital. Animals had been chewing at his face and chest for hours and the sheer horror of what was happening must have turned his mind. Most of his nose and cheeks had been eaten away and his wife was shocked by his appearance. At his bedside, she watched as her husband regained consciousness and began twitching and sobbing, before muttering nonstop gibberish. The body lived, but the Dalca she had married was gone forever. She wondered if it might have been better if he had died rather than have him live on in such a state.

Details of the cowardly attack on a respected public official were headline news for some days, but the police view was that it had probably been a revenge attack by someone Dalca had harmed under the previous communist regime, which had shown no respect for human rights. After seven days in hospital, the doctors could do no more and Dalca was sent home to be cared for by his wife. The newspapers reported that the commissar had received hospital treatment for his wounds and would now be at home recuperating on sick leave.

It was a sunny day and Madame Dalca decided to work in her vegetable garden. She placed a sun lounger on the front porch for her husband to relax his wounded leg and rest in the sun, where she could keep watch on him. After an hour battling with weeds and making regular checks on her husband, she decided to take a break and make coffee. She stretched her aching back and then walked slowly back to the house. Glancing towards the porch, she was horrified to see a large knife protruding from her husband's chest and after finding no pulse, she knew he was dead.

She recognised one of her own kitchen knives and could not believe that the killer had first entered her house and then callously stabbed her husband when she was working close by. After every five or six minutes bent over weeding, she had been straightening up to ease her back and check on her husband at the same time. The murderer would only have needed seconds to kill her man and she shuddered as she realised that if she had turned round and seen him, she would certainly have been killed as well.

Although she rarely drank alcohol, she poured herself a half glass of brandy to settle her nerves before calling the police.

After describing the killing, she then locked herself in the bathroom and stayed until she heard the police arrive. Once again, she watched as her husband was taken away in an ambulance, but this time there would be no return.

Balaclava man had passed a death sentence on Dalca and after reading the newspaper item, he was not prepared to have his victim live on for many years. Taking a bus to the outskirts of Bucharest, he walked to the Dalca house and after watching the woman in the garden, he chose a long-bladed knife from the kitchen. Waiting until the wife had made her regular check on her husband, he calmly moved up beside him, put a hand over his mouth and drove the knife down deep into the chest of the sleeping man, who died instantly. The knife pierced the heart and Dalca died without waking from his heavily drugged sleep.

With no evidence as to who had killed Dalca, or why and no obvious suspects, the police assured his wife that they would continue their investigations, but she knew that they had little hope of finding the assassin. His killer had already returned to Bucharest and was now planning how he would execute his next victim. Once again, he wanted to make it a long and excruciating death.

Chapter 6
Intrusion

Superintendent Larry James was speaking with Peter when Jack was shown into his office and as they shook hands, he expressed his opinion of the night incident.

"Morning, Jack, and congratulations on capturing those felons. Their clothes are new and my guess is they were bought locally and they could well be illegal immigrants. All four seem totally unconcerned about being arrested. Peter has already told you that none of them have spoken a word, nor did they speak when you tied them up I gather. I hope that there is not going to be another run of killings by maverick Hungarians."

"Good morning, Superintendent. I certainly hope this does not lead to more innocent deaths. Our last foreign visitors came armed and were quick to use their guns. These four beat my men, but did not want to kill them, probably because that would have brought an immediate police response. I think they were targeting me, or my business. So far, we have no idea why, since no-one has yet been making offers to take over our customers."

"We can charge them with assault and breaking and entering Jack, but since they don't seem to be UK citizens, they will eventually be handed over to the immigration authorities. Assault may be tricky to prove, since you knocked them down and tied them up, but there was the previous attack on your staff. My guess is that this is the beginning of something and we shall just have to be on our guard until we know who, or what we are dealing with. Our cities offer rich pickings to criminals and ex-military men from some of the Balkan states. What do you think, Peter?"

"Well, sir, we can take their mug shots and prints and if they do come back to Liverpool, we will know them and depending on any offence they may commit, we will charge them. Other than that Jack, we can't do much to help you."

Jack shook hands with both policemen and drove to the hospital to check on his two injured security men. Although bruised and in pain, they were glad to see him and accepted the attacks as part of their work risk. They welcomed the issue of helmets and working in pairs. He made no mention of his idea of issuing pepper sprays, since Greg would be responsible for briefings and training. Returning to his office, he telephoned his Trade Councils contact in Germany and spoke to him about pepper sprays. He was told that they used two types, one for use against brown bears in southern Germany and a more powerful version for humans, as used by the police and military. The first was legal and the second was not.

When he told Greg about the German pepper sprays, his friend explained what he had learned from his own research. The sprays were banned in the UK and although they had good relations with the police and any thugs, they sprayed were unlikely to complain, he had an alternative.

"You can buy a product called Farb-Gel in a can and when this is sprayed at face-level it should disorient the attacker, who will certainly have to wipe it from his eyes and then find his hands are blood red. The momentary shock should allow our men time to floor them and slip self-locking plastic handcuffs over their wrists. The handcuffs are made by Mil-Tec and are quite cheap. We can get both items together for around a tenner. The red dye on their faces and hands will last for seven days and make these guys easy to spot even if they do get away."

"I like it, Greg. It will give our boys an extra option and we stay within the law. Just go ahead and order what you need. What about asking Joe Devine to use his network of informers to check if there are any new crime gangs who have arrived in the city recently. They could be just beginning to make approaches and if they are migrants, they should stand out with their accents, especially if they are using muscle. The place is booming and most city centre businesses are doing well and would make tempting targets for some sort of local protection racket. I still can't understand why our men and sites were picked out, unless there is some sort of major assault planned to take over, or control major companies. We may be top of their list and will have to convince them that it won't work."

The next Hun-Al board meeting was due in Budapest in four weeks' time and Jack hoped that by then the construction of the rail link would be progressing well, provided that there were no unexpected problems with materials, or the local Roma people. He was in regular contact with Demeter on various company issues and knew he would soon learn about any threats to the mine, or new rail track.

The schools were on holiday and he had booked a three-day midweek break at a holiday camp near Penrith. After clearing his correspondence, he drove home to help Judy with the children. She was already packing for their early start on the drive north the next morning. After living in the French countryside, young Paul had picked up a surprising knowledge of the language through contact with the locals around the farm, as well as Hungarian from his mother, although his main language was now English. As the two small boys spent most of their time together, Leighton had now added a mixture of foreign phrases to his own vocabulary and Judy was concerned that it would affect his schoolwork. Jack was not as concerned because he believed that both boys were building a sound base to becoming multilingual.

Early the next morning, they drove off with plans to take full advantage of the heated pool, wave machine and water slides. Judy had recently fallen and was still suffering back pain and was happy to relax with baby Samantha in the comfortable central atrium.

The weather was warm and sunny and Jack hired bikes for himself and the two boys to explore the site and local countryside. Both boys had recently learned to swim in the local swimming club and Jack was happy to keep an eye on them as he sat on the side, out of splashing range and watched them play in the water.

Chapter 7
Consolidation

The rail tracks had been shipped north up the Danube on large barges pulled by a motorised mother vessel. They were now stacked in the storage yard of the refinery and work had already begun to clear a level pathway for laying the track to the mine. Fortunately, the land between the mine and refinery was fairly flat and should not require extensive preparation. Although heavy machinery was used for most of the work, there was some requirement for manual labourers, which provided work for men from the local Roma community.

As tracks were laid on the route to the mine, work was also begun at the refinery to build the structure, which would empty ore from incoming trucks and feed it to the processing area. An engine shed was also built to provide cover from the harsh winter weather for engineers servicing, or repairing the steam engine. V-shaped linking tracks were laid up to the shed to allow the engine to reverse, move forward, or change direction.

As the line began extending steadily towards the Roma village there were no setbacks either with the terrain, or the Roma people. Larjos Farkas, the engineer in charge, was beginning to feel more confident that it would be completed on time and on budget. The steam engine had also arrived and was now being used to pull two flatbed trucks carrying rail to the front of the line for siting. Larjos calculated that the railhead should reach the outskirts of the village in three weeks' time.

After another day of track laying, the steam engine returned to the refinery and reversed into the engine shed for the night and its boiler fire was raked and cleaned out. Early the next morning with steam up, it moved slowly forward from its shed along the linking track to join the line towards the Roma village. The train driver first checked that the lever showed the points were still connected from the previous night and increased speed. Suddenly, the engine lurched and then shuddered as it was derailed, but somehow managed to remain upright although its front wheels had left the track.

Climbing down from the cab, the engine driver walked across to the points lever and found that it still showed the connection to the engine shed. Larjos Farkas came running over to look for the cause of the derailment and was furious to find that it was deliberate. Someone had changed the points to seal the entry to the engine shed, dismantled the lever and replaced it to make it appear that the points to the engine shed were still connected. Heavy lifting gear would have to be brought from Budapest to raise the engine and the damaged track would need replacing.

Flatbed trucks were already loaded with rails and waiting to be hauled along the line for extending the railhead, but without the engine, the work was stopped. Farkas was convinced that the damage must be the work of the Roma. It only required points to be switched and bolts undone to refit the lever, indicating that the rails were still linked. Some of the villagers had already moved away to escape the noise and dust from the mine, but those who remained were determined to get the line diverted to protect their homes, or receive compensation for the loss of their houses. Farkas knew that his bosses would agree to neither of these options and he would have to improve security to protect the line as it progressed through the village.

When he was told about the derailment, Demeter quickly arranged another meeting with Boldo, who arrived at his home and was again accompanied by his silent Romanian visitor. Knowing the attitude of his fellow board members, he hoped to persuade Boldo to restrain those hotheads who wanted to cause trouble, which was bound to bring harsh reprisals from the government. Hungary badly needed foreign exchange income and the government would not tolerate obstruction by anyone, let alone a small group of Roma.

"Do you know that someone has derailed the company steam engine by changing the points, Boldo?"

"We have heard that it will not move along the rails and my people are being blamed, but I do not know if that is so. Many of my people are not happy about the noise of the mine and the rails which are coming to destroy our village. Some are already moving away from Dunakeszi, but I do not know if perhaps some of them did this before leaving."

"If that is so Boldo, then those who remain will suffer. I have spoken with Larjos Farkas, who has reported to Budapest that work on the rail line is stopped until the engine can be lifted back onto the line. I am only one against five government members on the board and they will decide what happens, whatever I say."

"My people are very unhappy that the mine has come and they will be angry if they are forced from their homes when they are crushed by your machines. I will tell them what you say, but I do not know if they will listen now."

"It might be possible to move rails by pulling the trucks along the line with horses and your people have dozens. If they help to keep work on the line going, perhaps I can persuade the other directors to accept that the engine was derailed by those who have now left the village."

Hearing this offer, Boldo looked at his colleague, who shrugged his shoulders, but gave no other indication as to his opinion. Demeter wondered just how much Hungarian the man could understand. Boldo agreed to talk to his people, but seeing the resigned expression on his face, Demeter had little hope that help would be provided as he watched the two men drive off. He had done all he could and it was now up to the Roma to cooperate, or face the consequences. Farkas was furious about the engine derailment and wanted to retaliate by immediately sending bulldozers into the Roma village to clear space for the rail line. Demeter managed to persuade him to wait and give Boldo a chance to organise teams of horses to move the rails.

As he drove back to his village, Boldo listened as his friend told him what must be done next and although he was concerned about taking such drastic action, he reluctantly agreed. A meeting of all the villagers was called and for over an hour they listened as the Romanian visitor convinced them that it was time to make a stand and force the government to give them equal treatment with other citizens. If they followed his directions, none of them would be arrested, or charged with any offences. The following morning, the teams of horses did not appear, nor did the Roma men who had been working at the mine, rail track, or refinery. Anxious to know what was happening, Demeter and

Farkas drove to the Roma village and found that every house was empty. All the people and their horses must have left during the night.

Although furious that he would not be getting horses to move his rails, Farkas was relieved that at least now he would avoid facing angry Roma as he began to clear a path through the village. As they were walking around the empty houses, Demeter received a telephone call from the foreman at the mine to report that there had been a break in during the night. He asked if anything had been taken and felt a cold chill when he learned that two boxes of explosives and detonators had been stolen. The situation now looked as though it was running out of control and there could well be serious injuries, or even fatalities. He decided that it was time to update his friend Jack about the first indications of a Roma campaign to disrupt the Hun-Al mine operations. He knew that there had been attacks on some of Jack's security men in Liverpool, but his friend was sure that precautions taken would prevent further incidents and he was prepared to fly to Hungary if he was needed.

Chapter 8
Vengeance

After his promotion to sergeant-major on his return from the expedition to Budestin village in northern Romania, Dinescu thought for the first time that he felt grateful to the Tigani people, who for him always seemed to be either begging or stealing. Pleased with the way he had dealt with the troublesome villagers at Budestin, his superiors had shown their gratitude by giving him his promotion. After fifteen years of service, he was proud of his progress after being recruited as a barely educated farm worker.

He had been trying to sell his car and replace it with a more modern and reliable model, but after weeks of offering it for sale on the barracks noticeboard, he had no enquiries. Anxious to sell before it cost him even more money in repairs, he decided to place an advertisement in the local newspaper. He received four replies, of which three were near the barracks and one required him to take the car outside Bucharest to a farm near Lake Pantelimon.

After showing the car to each of the nearest contacts, the poor condition of the bodywork and noisy engine resulted in three negative responses. Even when he reduced his asking price they were still not interested. Reluctantly, Dinescu was forced to agree to meet Mr Butaco on his farm, who was looking for a cheap, but reliable car. If he agreed to buy the car, the farmer told Dinescu that he would drive him to the town of Pantelimon, which had a good rail link to Bucharest. He also suggested bringing the car with a full tank of petrol as part of the deal.

Dinescu was able to use his free time on Saturday to make the drive to the northeast from the barracks and was glad that it was a fine day to help in finding his way. The farmer had given him very good directions, but after making a wrong turn he stopped to speak to a group of workers in a field and was given more directions to the isolated farm. Finally, he reached a crossroad and saw a signpost with a new board indicating the dirt track to the Butaco farm. There were potholes and stone outcrops in the rough track, which ran for at least a mile through neglected fields before the farm buildings became visible.

The farmer was outside working on a newly raked plot beside a large barn. When he saw the car approaching, he waved and began walking towards the farmhouse. Dinescu parked the car and then shook hands with the farmer, who invited him inside the kitchen for coffee. The farmer was wearing a woolly cap pulled down over his forehead and ears and a faded anorak. He was bearded and had a bushy moustache. He walked very slowly and Dinescu guessed the man was in his early fifties. He complained that the winds could get very cold in this flat and open area and it badly affected his ears. After inviting Dinescu to sit down at a table, he bustled around behind him as he was making the coffee.

Suddenly, Dinescu felt a hard blow to the back of his head and everything went black as he collapsed to the stone floor unconscious. When he awoke an hour later and opened his eyes, he could see grey clouds passing above him in the sky and found that he was lying on his back in some sort of trench in the earth. He could move his legs, but his arms were tightly bound to his side. Looking around, he saw that the earth walls around him were about four feet high and only slightly wider than his shoulders. Apart from an aching head, he had no other injuries and no idea why the farmer had attacked him, unless he wanted to steal the car.

There were some small stones in the earth beneath him, which were digging into his back and he used his legs to try to lift his body and move them sideways. After some minutes of lifting and nudging, he managed to move most of the bigger stones across to his sides, but he was exhausted by the effort. The farmer suddenly appeared above him and Dinescu saw he was holding an old wooden door in his arms.

"What is this all about Mr Butaco and why have you tied me up in this trench?"

He received no answer from the farmer, who callously dropped the door on top of the soldier. It fell on his face and body, so that he was stunned momentarily by the heavy blow. Reopening his eyes, he began to panic as he found that he could no longer see the sky and was in darkness, apart from some dim light seeping past the sides of the door. Next, he heard the rattle of more stones and earth thrown down as they fell on the door above him. As the work continued, the light no longer permeated through and he was left helpless and in complete darkness. He realised he was being buried alive and he began to shout and scream as he pleaded with Butaco to let him out.

On the remote farm, only his captor heard his screams, which had no effect on the man shovelling down earth to completely fill the trench and bury Dinescu. Once the earth was level with the top, the surface was carefully raked over to match that of the recently dug surrounding plot. The heavy earth filling reduced Dinescu's screams to a faint murmur and as the air under the protecting door was used up, that too would eventually stop. After looking carefully around to be sure that there was no indication of the pit lying beneath the surface, the man walked back to the farmhouse.

Inside the house, he made his way down to the cellar where the real farm owner Butaco was tied up and blindfolded. The thick stone walls would have made it difficult for Butaco to hear the conversations in his kitchen and he had carefully said very little to the soldier. It was unlikely that he would hear the screams from Dinescu in his burial pit and he had cut the phone line to the farm. He spoke to the farmer.

"You will find a kitchen knife on your right hand side so that you can use it to free yourself. You must count slowly to one hundred before searching for the knife and you will then save your own life. If you do not wait, remember that I may be watching and I will then slit your throat from ear to ear. Do you want to die?"

The farmer shook his head vigorously and muttered through his gag. Satisfied that the man would do as he was told, the assassin walked out to the shabby Dacia car and put his knapsack on the passenger seat. After checking that there were no strangers, or vehicles in sight, he removed his woolly cap and peeled off the false beard and moustache, which he bundled up with the faded anorak and tossed into the back of the car. He then began his journey to the far side of Lake Pantelimon and parked near the shore. After carefully checking that there was no one in sight, he opened his knapsack, pulled out walking boots and outdoor clothing and put them on. He had deliberately parked in a deserted area and he then used a tube to siphon petrol from the tank into an old jerry can.

After throwing petrol over the inside and outside of the car, he reached inside and picked up the old anorak, which he also soaked with petrol. There was plenty of driftwood lying at the lakeside and he found himself a long branch and tied the anorak to its end. Taking no chances, he first lit some dried grass and twigs and used the fire to ignite the anorak, before using the branch to toss it at the car. With a roar, the car exploded into a fireball and although he had flung himself to the ground, he still felt the blast of hot air. Satisfied that his mission was completed, he began the long walk to the nearest railway station for his journey back to Bucharest.

He could easily have killed Dinescu in the farm kitchen, but he had carefully planned to have his prey completely off guard so that he could overpower him and then make him face a lingering death. After earlier touring the chosen area, he had identified the remote farm and discovered that Butaco was an old man who was well known, but independent and living on his own. Once he had arranged for Dinescu to drive to the farm, he had taken a bus to the nearest village and then made the long walk to the farm. After knocking on the door, he had pushed Butaco inside, overpowered him and tied him up in the cellar. He then dug up a sizeable area alongside the barn, as well as the deep grave for his victim. Newly dug soil for the grave would have been conspicuous and he had dug over a large area to make it blend in until the soldier had died. He doubted that the body would ever be found.

Dropping the wooden door on top of his victim had provided an air pocket beneath, which avoided having him quickly suffocate when the trench was filled with earth. Butaco might not bother to report his confinement in his cellar to the police, since neither he, nor his property had been harmed and his phone line had been cut. If he did make a report, Butaco would describe his attacker as a bearded old man and he would not have seen the car or Dinescu. He would wonder why some of his land had been turned over and raked, but might not mention it to the police. If the farmer did tell the police that some of his land had been dug over, there was little hope of rescue for the buried soldier.

The burning car would certainly be noticed and reported to the police at some point. When it was identified as belonging to Dinescu, who would have been reported missing, it might be assumed that he had been killed. Any search for his body was more likely to be in the lake area near the burned-out car. If the police linked the farm incident with the burned-out car, the only possible clue to Dinescu's grave was the newly dug plot at the farm and it would by then contain his dead body.

Inside his dark hole, Dinescu tried to contain his flaring panic and, after a tremendous struggle, was able to slowly raise his knees and lift the wooden door and earth above it, which was not yet compacted. The earth on the surface rippled gently, but there was no one to see it. The farmer found that his house phone would not work and angered by his confinement, he decided he would walk to the nearest house to contact the police. In his haste to make his complaint, he hurried from his house and failed to notice the newly dug plot near his barn. At the end of the long lane leading to his farm, he was surprised to see a new sign with Butaco on it and assumed that local officials had placed it. When he eventually returned home after telephoning the police from a local store with details of his brief imprisonment, he was convinced that his long walk was a waste of time and effort, since the police seemed to think it was some sort of prank.

As he returned to his house, he noticed the newly dug area near his barn and guessed that the work must have been done by his attacker. Perhaps the man had just wanted some exercise. Nothing appeared to have been planted and it never occurred to him that someone had been buried beneath. Deciding that he might as well benefit from the work and having a sack full of old potatoes, he planted them in the newly dug area.

Chapter 9

Assassination

The Randil family enjoyed the holiday break and Jack spent much of the time in the pool teaching Leighton and Paul how to dive. The boys soon grew confident as they floated and swam in the water and Jack knew that he would have to make regular visits to the local swimming pool on their return home.

There had been no further attacks on his security men as they completed their night rounds. Jack wondered if this was because the culprits had been caught and the attacks would resume when new men had been recruited. The respite allowed time for Greg to issue the new items. All security men were given colour sprays and plastic cuffs as well as protective helmets. By having them working in pairs, Greg believed he had taken the necessary precautions against more night attacks. There were no incidents during the following week and no attempts by competitive companies to poach Randil customers.

A week later, Randil security men on their night rounds called at a large manufacturing company and parked their van at the rear entrance, before beginning their patrol of the buildings. Having completed their checks with no signs of any intruders, the two men were walking along the access corridor to their van when they heard a loud explosion. It seemed to come from the entrance area and they began running towards it. When they opened the outer door, they were faced with a wall of flames coming from their van. Although it was parked roughly eight feet from the building, they were concerned that with the intensity of the fire, it could spread to the building itself. After ringing the fire brigade and their supervisor, they collected fire extinguishers from inside the building and used another exit to approach their burning van from the outside.

The heat of the fire prevented them from getting close enough to spray it and they were forced to stand aside as the vehicle burned. The fire brigade reached the scene within fifteen minutes and hosed down the vehicle and blistering entrance door and windows. Greg and their supervisor arrived at the same time and were followed by the factory safety officer, who had been called by Greg. The building door and windows nearest the fire would need repainting, or replacing, but the van itself with tools and equipment was a total write off.

The attacks on Randil security staff and arrest of the four intruders had already been featured in the *Liverpool Echo* and was now followed by a report of the arson attack on a Randil van. The fire brigade had found that the petrol cap had been removed and they believed some sort of fuse had been used to ignite the fuel. The article implied that the attacks were directed against Randil Building Services and Jack was concerned that the bad publicity might have an adverse effect on the business.

Jack and Greg met with their big friend Joe Devine, the next morning to discuss the situation, which was now becoming more serious. Not only were Jack's employees being threatened, but there could also be concern by his customers that Jack's company was not safe to employ. He realised that he must find the culprits quickly, or face losing a large part of his company security operations.

Joe had already asked his citywide contacts to check on any newcomers who had been hiring muscle, or starting up new protection rackets, but so far, he had learned nothing. Jack was convinced that the attacks were being carried out by a foreign group, who had recently arrived in Liverpool. The four captured thugs had still not spoken and would shortly be transferred to the immigration authorities, who were unlikely to be able to keep them for long.

Coffee was brought in for the men and Jack began the discussion.

"We were able to put a stop to the attacks on our staff, but unless we also put guards on our vans, they will be vulnerable. Whoever these people are, they have already begun making us look helpless and hold the initiative. We have to wait for them to make a mistake, or show themselves before we can begin to retaliate."

As ever Joe Devine, his ex RSM Marine friend, was happy to do all he could to help.

"That's how I see it Jack, but when we do need to take them on, I can get you all the trained ex-military men you need. They are all keen to protect the colleagues you have working for you. What does your pal Peter Kershaw in the police think is happening?"

"They are still sensitive about our involvement with the explosions at the Town Hall and Southport marsh area, but are as keen as we are to trace any more foreign visitors who might be here to cause trouble. Remember that some of their own people were murdered by those fanatics as well Joe."

Shaking his head as he remembered how he had been shot during the confrontation, Joe agreed.

"Yes, it was a nasty business for us all and none of us wants to go through that again. What about that London crime boss who blew himself up, Marik was his name, wasn't it?"

"I wondered about that as well, but with Marik dead, I should think his business will probably be taken over by the other London gangs and since Marik had no number two, there is unlikely to be anyone to step into his shoes."

Listening to his friends speculating on possible groups who might want to attack the company, Greg remembered another killer who had hated Jack and his friends.

"What about Roger Donnelly and his IRA contacts. He nearly blew up your warehouse after you shot his buddies. He has family back in Ireland and they may have decided to make you pay for interfering in their operations in the city?"

Jack agreed that there could be retaliation from relatives back in Ireland, but he thought that the attacks would be made directly against him, rather than his business. Without more information they would just have to be on their guard and look for some sign of those behind the attacks.

As the three men finished their discussion and went off to their respective offices, a tall, thickset man was making his way through passport control after his five-hour flight from Cyprus. He was in a bad mood after being told by his leaders in Larnaca to transfer his special talents to Merseyside, which he had heard was a big, noisy and cold area. For the past eight years he had enjoyed a warm Mediterranean climate and was shown respect wherever he went, as well as having access to dozens of attractive young women who were always eager to please him. After the biting cold and austerity of the Russian capital, it was like living in paradise. He had worked hard to help build the business from its early days and believed he had earned the right to enjoy the benefits. Instead, he was given the choice of working in Liverpool, or being sent back to Russia.

After showing the taxi driver the hotel address written on some paper, he checked in and ate in the plain and dimly lit dining room. The food was tasteless and the waiter appeared to have little interest in him, or his order. Ahtoh Kovalik was forty-eight years old and realised that in spite of his years of service and experience, he was losing out to younger men who were desperate to prove themselves. Pushing aside his unfinished meal, he returned to his room to put on warm clothes for his first look around the city centre.

After only a few minutes walking along the busy street, he found himself outside the Tropicana Bistro and looking through the plate glass windows with ornamental metal guards, it looked inviting. He pushed through the double doors and was impressed by the red leather seats on stools and booths, with chrome edgings. He used his bulk to get a seat at the very busy bar and was irritated that the barmaid did not immediately come to him for his order. Generally, people recognised who, or what he was and he was given space and first-class service. As the barmaid was passing him for the third time, he grabbed her arm and ordered whisky. The young woman was annoyed and turned to tell him to let go of her arm, but when she looked into the dark eyes and saw the broad face and thick black hair, she decided it was wiser to say nothing. The woman was popular and the regular drinkers stared at the stranger, and were annoyed by his bad behaviour and manners.

Ahtoh was unaware of the disapproval his behaviour had caused and emptying his glass in one gulp, he held it out in front of the barmaid for a refill. When he had emptied his second glass, he turned to the man alongside and muttered, "*Nipthras*." The man shrugged his shoulders and realising his mistake, Ahtoh said, "Want lavabo." Recognising the words, the man pointed to the far corner of the room and Ahtoh patted the man on the shoulder before making his way to relieve himself. When he returned to the bar, a man was sitting on his stool and his empty glass had been removed. Furious to have his place taken by another and already in a bad mood because of his unjust transfer to Liverpool, he grabbed the man's shoulder with one large hand and yanked him from the stool so that he sprawled on the floor.

Quickly getting to his feet, the man shouted and threw a punch at Ahtoh, which he blocked automatically, before smashing his own large fist into the man's stomach and then hitting him on the chin. The man collapsed on the floor and two of his friends then attacked Ahtoh, who absorbed their blows as he drove his fists into each and laid them out. The room fell silent and no one was prepared to attack the big angry man with black hair. Realising that he was drawing unwanted attention and could be in trouble with the police, he walked quickly from the bar. Once outside, he could not remember which direction to take to return to his hotel and mistakenly walked in the opposite direction. After twenty minutes, he found himself beyond the brightly lit city centre in a quiet part of Liverpool, with unlit buildings and few people. Realising his mistake, he turned back to retrace his steps.

He then saw that there were four, or possibly five darkly dressed men moving towards him and knew that he would have to fight to survive. They had long sticks in their hands and it was only when the first blow landed on his shoulders, that he realised they were iron stakes. In the bar he had manhandled and shamed three members of the Croxteth Young Guns gang, and they had now come back with reinforcements to take their revenge. Ahtoh had no chance to strike more than a few blows before he was beaten down to the ground and kicked and hammered until his body was just a bloody heap on the pavement. The few people who saw the attack hurried to the other side of the road and took care to see nothing of the attackers.

On Wednesday night after their regular squash game, Jack and Peter Kilshaw were sipping their beers in the Leisure Centre bar where they were joined by Greg Ridd. Peter told them about a foreigner who started a fight in a city centre bar with three members of a local gang the previous night. A passing police car had surprised the attackers, who quickly ran off as the two policemen tried to help the victim on the ground. An ambulance took the badly injured man to hospital, but he died before recovering consciousness. A boarding pass stub in his pocket showed that he had flown in from Cyprus. Surprisingly his passport was in an inside pocket of his coat and showed that the man was Russian.

They were all aware that the Russian Mafia dominated crime in Cyprus and wondered if the dead man was connected to the four silent men who had attacked the Randil security teams. If the Cyprus criminals were now targeting Liverpool, it would be a major threat and the three men dreaded to think of the consequences. Whatever had led the Russian to brawl with the gang members in the city centre bar, it could have given them an early warning and the opportunity to concentrate their investigations on recent arrivals from Cyprus with Russian passports. It was possible that they would arrive illegally by boat, or use false passports, but the murdered man had flown in by Cyprus Air and perhaps other members of the gang would do the same. Now they knew what to look for and would make an immediate start.

Jack told them that he would draft a letter, giving details of their suspicions and send it to their contact in each company where Randil provided security services. Peter was not happy about possibly alerting the Russians, but Jack convinced him that it could flush them out. There would certainly be details of the murder of a Russian national in the *Liverpool Echo* after starting a fight in the bar and he would simply draw a line to the four foreign thugs who were in detention. He needed to protect his business and keep his customers informed of the threat if the Russians were able to establish a major operation in the city.

Still not happy, Peter persuaded Jack to wait until he had checked with the Cyprus police whether Ahtoh Kovalik was a member of the Russian Mafia in Cyprus. If he was, the link with the four thugs would be very much stronger. The following morning Peter rang to confirm that Ahtoh was a well-known and active member of the Mafia and had been for many years. Jack sent his letter to all his security customers and to his employees. Joe Devine's contacts began searching for strangers in the crime world, in cooperation with the Merseyside police.

With the very likely possibility that Russian Mafia were active in Liverpool, Jack and Greg arranged to meet for coffee at Joe Devine's café in his Fitness Club to consider the threat.

Having sent out his letter, Jack hoped it would alert people to the new dangers and also that Randils were seeking information, but Joe thought there was something he could do which would help to trace the foreign criminals.

"Some of the Croxteth Young Guns use my gym to build their muscles and get together in the café afterwards. They are good customers; never give me any trouble and we sometimes pass the time of day together. Why don't I mention the item in the paper about the Russian killed in the city and tell them my city contacts think he was part of the Russian Mafia moving in from Cyprus. They won't want competition and if the two mobs take each other on, it makes it better for us."

Greg thought this would add more eyes and ears to locate the Russians, but could also lead to a turf war in the city. Jack had his own view of the idea.

"The local boys are going to fight to hold on to their business against the Russians sooner, or later. All Joe would be doing is giving them an early warning of their new competitors. Go ahead Joe, but be very careful, we don't want them shooting the messenger."

Chapter 10
Sabotage

The explosives, together with drills and other small tools were stored in a specially constructed building without windows and fitted with a steel door secured by a heavy padlock. The mine manager showed Demeter how the padlock had been ripped from the door for the thieves to gain access. Only the explosives and fuses had been taken, although tools and other items could have been sold if the break in was a normal robbery. The thieves had known exactly what they needed for their purposes.

Demeter telephoned Radics with details of the break in. His fellow director was initially angry that there had been another attempt by locals to disrupt their mining operations. Then the full implications of explosives in the hands of those responsible dawned on him.

"I will not allow these people to interfere in our plans and protection will be arranged for the rail line and mine, which could be targets. You persuaded me to let them work in the mine and this is the result. Anyone caught damaging our operation will spend many years in jail."

Having had his say, Radics slammed the phone down and Demeter thought about having another meeting with Boldo, but remembered the village was deserted. Frustrated by the continuing problems he vowed to find a new location for Boldo and his people. It was very likely that the silent companion was the real leader behind the attacks. It would be impossible to question him unless he could get help from someone who spoke Romanian. He knew he should have told Radics about the stranger in the Roma village who watched and listened, but said nothing. Unfortunately, the commissar had been so angry that Demeter was forced to hold the phone away from his ear during the tirade and had little chance to say very much. He knew he must do something to prevent further trouble, but even with security guards watching the vulnerable parts of their operations, the Roma could always find ways to avoid them. The Hun-Al company should be bringing prosperity and foreign exchange to his country, but instead it was creating trouble and possible deaths.

The next board meeting would be held in just over a week and he was sure Jack Randil would be able to advise him on convincing the Roma and Radics to find a compromise in their attitudes. When he returned to the refinery the crane had arrived and lifted the wheels of the engine back to the rail tracks. The boiler was fired up and the trucks loaded with rail track would soon be on the way to the railhead, which would then be moving nearer to the abandoned Roma village. Although there would now be no villagers to create harassment, Demeter was still worried that there was going to be more trouble.

After repeated attempts on his life, his fiancée Theresa had made him promise to telephone her each evening at 8 pm so that they could exchange news on their day and she would be reassured that he was safe. On her next holiday from her studies at Durham University, they had arranged to meet in Budapest and he planned to show her the Pusztai mansion and explain his plan to restore it to its old glory. He made his regular telephone call.

Hearing the strain in his voice, Theresa knew that all was not well with the mine.

"You seem worried my love, are you having any problems?"

Demeter briefly described the difficulties with the local Roma people, but failed to mention the theft of explosives. Theresa was sympathetic with the families being forced from their homes and urged Demeter to help them.

"Hungary is struggling to recover from Russian dominance my darling and democracy is still in its infancy here, unlike in Britain. I will do what I can, but the government is making the major decisions in line with their policy. Also, Roma people are not considered full citizens because they wander from country to country and do not usually have permanent homes."

Her holiday visit was less than a month away and she hoped that Demeter and her Uncle Jack would be able to find some way of helping the Roma people, which did not conflict with government policy. As he switched off his phone, Demeter believed that Theresa was wishing for the impossible.

At the police station near Lake Pantelimon, the telephone call from the farmer Butaco was regarded as ramblings from an old fool by the policeman who took down his statement. He filed the report, but with few resources he did not expect that it would even justify a visit to the farm, since there was neither theft, nor injury. The affair would certainly have been quickly forgotten, except for another report regarding a burned-out car near the edge of the lake. Two policemen were sent to examine it and decided that it was arson. They made a note of the registration number and engine number to check ownership and reported back to the station. The registration number was traced to a Sergeant Dinescu at the Bucharest barracks.

When the barracks was contacted, the police were informed that the sergeant-major was off duty, but he would be informed when he returned. When he failed to report for duty the following day, his officer became concerned about Dinescu. After being told that his burned-out car had been found many miles away at Lake Pantelimon, he issued a request for a search to be carried out in the area. The newly appointed police officer in charge at Pantelimon station was Lieutenant Petru Bumbesco, who had recently been transferred from Bucharest HQ. He meticulously read all reports and was puzzled by the odd story told by the farmer Butaco.

Bumbesco arranged for a search of the lake area, but also telephoned the barracks to ask why Dinescu would have visited the remote neighbourhood. When he learned that the visit was to sell the car, the Lieutenant asked if the name of the buyer was known. A colleague remembered Dinescu complaining about having to drive so far to show the car to some farmer called Butaco. The name was familiar and linked with the odd report from the farmer. Bumbesco and another policeman drove to the farm to interview Butaco. After hearing his story, the two officers examined the ground near the farmhouse and found oil stains and car tracks. Since Butaco did not have a car, it could only have come from Dinescu's Dacia.

It appeared that a bearded old man had overpowered and locked up Butaco. When Dinescu arrived at the farm, he would probably have pretended to be the farmer and then taken the car, probably after killing Dinescu to get it. He must have taken his body in the car to dispose of it, but why do all this and then burn the car and why drive it to the lake in the first place? Bumbesco realised that the target must have been the soldier and not the car. No body was found in the burned-out car, nor in the shallow lake itself. He would continue his search for the body, but inform the army authorities of the likely murder and ask them to investigate possible enemies who would want to kill the sergeant-major.

As he was standing outside the run-down farmhouse and neglected outbuildings with the farmer, he took a long look around the buildings and surrounding fields and noticed some newly dug earth near the barn. The area stood out, where none of the surrounding fields had been worked on for some time. It seemed odd and he asked Butaco what had been planted. The farmer told him he had just put in a crop of potatoes, but never thought to mention that the digging had been done by his bearded visitor, although he had thought it strange that the man needed the exercise.

Chapter 11
Destruction

Demeter spent a full day driving his Kawasaki quad bike across his land and covered all the likely places to try to discover where the Roma people had fled. As it grew dark, he was forced to give up, but had found no trace of them. As he was making his search, the train was used to move more rails to the end of the line, which would allow track-laying to extend to the outskirts of the deserted Roma village. As promised, there was extra security at the mine and the refinery in accordance with orders from Commissar Radics.

Two days passed with no sign of any of the Roma people after their mass exodus from their homes. There were no further incidents to cause disruption of the mining operation and everyone was beginning to think that the problem had solved itself. Nevertheless, Demeter was still concerned about the reasons for the theft of explosives and instructed his staff to remain on the alert.

In the early hours of the following morning, the noise of a loud explosion disturbed the sleep of the local population and the sound seemed to come from the direction of the deserted Roma village. Security staff piled into a lorry and drove towards the source of the noise. When they arrived at the railhead, they found that the stack of rails left alongside the line for installation had been turned into a heap of twisted metal by the explosion. As they were examining the damage and checking that there were no booby traps laid under the rail line itself, they heard the noise of two more explosions and this time they seemed to come from the refinery area. They later learned that half an hour after the team of security men drove off from their main base at the refinery, two guards who had remained behind to protect the area were overpowered and blindfolded before being tied up.

Guessing that they had been deliberately drawn away from the more important targets at the refinery, the security team hurried to climb into their lorry to investigate the new explosions. When they arrived back at the refinery, they saw that two steel towers, which had supported the conveyor belt and loading chutes had been toppled by the explosions. They would have to be rebuilt before any more ore could be fed into the refinery processing plant. Dynamite had been placed under their concrete bases to cause the damage.

As he looked at the jumbled mess and appreciated that his production had been brought to a standstill, Larjos Farkas could feel the cold sweat breaking out on his body. With the extra security men he had been given, he had unwisely told Commissar Radics that there was now no threat to his production operations. None of his workers, or the security staff had been injured, but Larjos was less concerned about them than he was about his own reputation and future.

As he was looking at the damage, he heard the distant sound of yet another explosion and this time it appeared to come from the mine itself. Determined to show that he was in control and to regain the initiative, he first organised a team of men to begin clearing the fallen steel structures and then set off to see for himself the damage, which had probably been carried out at the mine. When he arrived, everything appeared to be normal, except that the massive digger on its caterpillar treads was missing. Seeing a group of men at the far side of the open cast mine, he hurried over to speak with them.

The foreman explained that the digger had been tearing ore out of the steep sides of the opencast mine and loading it into a large truck alongside. Suddenly, the steep side of the mine above the digger exploded and tons of ore and earth cascaded down and buried both the digger and the lorry. Since the digger and lorry drivers were both inside their steel cabs, he hoped that they would soon be able to dig them out unharmed, but it would be some time before extraction could be resumed. Tons of earth would have to be cleared and then the digger and lorry would have to be hosed down and any mechanical damage repaired. Larjos estimated that ore production could be stopped for at least a week and more rail track would be needed.

Demeter arrived and received an account of the situation from the foreman. He was already aware of the damage at the railhead and refinery when he approached Larjos and saw that the man was looking shocked and dejected.

"This was a well-planned operation Larjos, to show us that the mining operation is vulnerable and could be brought to a permanent standstill at any time. At least they made sure that your workers were not harmed. Your foreman thinks the drivers should be safe inside their cabs."

"I always knew that those damned Roma would cause us trouble and they are going to have to pay for doing all this damage. Commissar Radics will arrest the lot of them."

"I doubt that Larjos, since I spent all day yesterday looking for them and there were no Roma anywhere in the area. You can't arrest people who are not here, or charge them. If they are responsible, then they are also pretty smart. Or perhaps, they have a cunning leader to direct them and it cannot be Boldo."

Listening to Demeter, Larjos paled as he realised that with no one else to blame, the commissar would vent his full fury on him and he would be very lucky to keep his position as manager. Demeter was thinking about the silent Romanian who had been with Boldo at their meetings and whom he suspected was orchestrating the campaign against the mine. It might be cheaper to compensate the Roma for destroying their homes, instead of paying for a large security team and repairing the damage already done, which could become far greater. Radics had dismissed his suggestions at the Board Meeting because, like most Hungarians, he considered the Roma people inferior and incapable of fighting back. They should call an emergency Board Meeting as soon as possible, since this was certainly not the case with the Roma in Dunakeszi.

It would be half term break at Durham University in just two weeks and Theresa had already booked her flight to Budapest. If the situation at the mine worsened, possibly because of the hard-line attitude that he anticipated from Commissar Radics, he would have to insist that Theresa should cancel the visit to keep her away from danger.

Chapter 12
Preparation

Joe Devine watched two young men make their way to his gymnasium and spend their usual two hours working out on the weights and fitness machines. He sat down in the café where they were bound to pass him and drank a coffee from his usual pint-sized mug whilst reading the evening edition of the *Liverpool Echo*. One of the men stopped alongside his table with a friendly grin on his face.

"Hello Joe, the coffee must be really good if you can drink it from a mug that size."

"Now, now lads, you know it's one of the best brews in the city, which is why you come here. Sit down. Would you like coffee, or anything else?"

Both men sat down and asked for coffee, as they continued to wipe the sweat from their faces after their workout. Pointing at the opened newspaper, one of the men asked if there was anything special that Joe was reading. Joe told him that he was looking to see if there was any more information about the big Russian guy killed in the city centre. Seeing the sudden interest in the man's eyes, Joe explained that his pal Jack Randil suspected that the Russian Mafia was responsible for attacks on his security men. He went on to tell them that Jack was concerned that they might be trying to operate in Liverpool by targeting his security business. In the meantime, he was keeping his eyes and ears open to help his friend.

"What makes Jack Randil think they are Russian Mafia Joe?"

"He and his men caught four foreigners who were trying to ambush them at one of their customer sites and handed them over to the police. None of them have spoken a word yet, but then this Russian flies in from Cyprus and causes trouble and you know how the Russians have taken over drugs, prostitution and gambling in Cyprus. Jack thinks they now want to start operating in Liverpool."

The two men looked at each other and slowly drank their coffee as they asked if Joe had any other information about Russians in the city. He told them he was putting the word around and if he heard anything, he would let them know and perhaps they would do the same for him. They promised they would let him know if they heard anything about foreigners and one of the men said he had to visit the loo. As he was walking back, Joe saw that he was using his mobile phone to have a long conversation. Joe guessed that his information was being passed on. After finishing their coffee, the two men wasted no time in getting back to their car. Watching the car race out of his car park, Joe made a phone call to Jack Randil to tell him about his chat with two of the Young Guns gang and that the message had probably been passed on.

Kirill Lopatin had been a serving officer in the KGB when the USSR broke up and along with many others, he had decided it was time to leave and use his skills in the many burgeoning criminal organisations where there were rich rewards. Having served in the USA, Spain and the UK, he spoke fluent English and Spanish and had learned to blend in with his surroundings with ease. He had been told to set up a new operation in Liverpool and for three months had studied the area, before asking for four trained enforcers to join him in building the new operation.

He had decided to start by establishing a protection service, which required potential customers to be made aware of the violent repercussions which would follow if they refused to pay. He considered that the Liverpool police were too thinly spread to be a serious problem and had studied the Randil security service, which used trained ex-servicemen and could be a threat to his plans. He decided to deal with Randil security men first to show that they were unable to protect properties against his own men. The security business was controlled by an ex-army sergeant and his boss, who was an ex-army corporal and Kirill did not anticipate too much trouble from them. He was not aware that the ex-army sergeant had served with Jack in the paratroops during the Falklands conflict and both had later been involved in training troops in unarmed combat and infiltration. He realised after the early success that he would now have to step up his activities with four of his men overpowered and handed over to the police.

Ahtoh Kovalik was surplus to requirements in the Cyprus operation, which was now well established and required subtlety instead of muscle. The man was a tough and experienced enforcer and when it was suggested that he was available, Kirill had asked for him to be sent to Liverpool. Unfortunately, Ahtoh had grown used to his comfortable Cyprus lifestyle and considered that his past contributions entitled him to refuse the move. When it was made clear that his choice was Liverpool, or a return to Moscow, he had grudgingly chosen Liverpool.

Carrying a big chip on his shoulder, on arriving in Liverpool, he stupidly drank too much, started a brawl in a bar and was killed. Things were not going to plan and Kirill knew that he must very quickly show that he could succeed. He must choose between continuing to attack the Randil men, or punish those responsible for killing Ahtoh and show that he was the toughest operator in the city. Since his man had been very publicly killed by local gang members, he decided to take revenge on the killers. First, he would have to learn all he could about those responsible for Ahtoh's killing. Past experience had taught him that asking too many questions amongst the locals raised unwelcome interest. Instead, he steered conversations so that he gathered snippets of information, which he then pieced together. After visiting coffee bars, cafés and pubs and sharing drinks, cigarettes, or newspapers, his friendly and unassuming style had brought him the details he wanted.

He had been told that Ahtoh had been killed by the Young Guns and he even learned the names of the gang members roughed up by Ahtoh in the Tropicana Bistro. The gang was involved in providing protection, prostitution and drugs. If he could destroy them, he would have his revenge and be in a strong position to take over their established criminal activities.

The letter sent to customers by Jack Randil had been picked up by an alert *Liverpool Echo* reporter. In an editorial titled *'Foreign Criminals Invade City'*, he linked the attacks on Randil security staff by foreign thugs with the fight in the city centre bar started by a newly arrived Russian Mafia member, who was later killed. Reading this, Kirill was sure that the police would be checking on Russians arriving in Liverpool and when asking for more men to be sent, he specified that they should arrive separately and at varied entry points. As soon as they all reached Liverpool, he would begin his attacks on the locals who had killed Ahtoh.

During the next two weeks, the Randil Security team experienced no problems and although they continued to operate in two-man teams, their general routine had slowly returned to normal. Alerted to the possible threat to their city operations, the Young Guns gang had warned their members to be on the lookout for newly arrived Russians. They also offered a reward to any of their customers who provided them with information on the presence of the unwelcome intruders.

Moving slowly, but cautiously Kirill found accommodation for his steadily increasing team members in pairs in apartment blocks in the many run-down areas on the outskirts of the city. Two of the six men he was being sent were able to speak reasonable English, but with a pronounced accent. As he waited for his men to arrive, Kirill began building up information on the regular movements of the two Young Gang members who were manhandled by Ahtoh in the Tropicana Bistro bar. He also used the time to plan his revenge attacks on the Young Guns.

At Pantelimon in Romania, after making no progress in finding the body of the missing soldier Dinescu, Lieutenant Bumbesco drove to the army base at Bucharest to speak to the man's commanding officer and colleagues. When he heard that Dinescu had been promoted for successfully carrying out a raid on a Roma village ordered by Commissar Dalca, he immediately recognised the link between their deaths. It was common knowledge that the commissar despised the Roma people. It seemed likely that both men had been killed by Roma in revenge for the raid. A young boy and an old woman had been shot and because of inter marriages, many Roma were related and were likely to have blood ties with the victims.

Bumbesco had been stationed in Bucharest when Dalca had been rescued from the forest after his horrific experience. Someone wanted the commissar to suffer a long and painful death, but he survived, only to be stabbed when his wife was working in the garden nearby. If Dinescu had been killed by the same people, it was likely that he too would have been made to suffer a lingering death. The murderer, or murderers must be from the village of Budestin, which was destroyed by Dinescu and his men. Unfortunately, the inhabitants were now scattered amongst many other Roma villages and would be difficult to trace. Perhaps, he could persuade his superiors to send someone to the Budestin area to investigate and preferably the man chosen should have Roma roots.

A report and recommendations were sent to Bucharest Police HQ and Bumbesco was waiting for a response. Meantime, he decided to pay another visit to the farm and have another interview with the farmer Butaco. The farm had to be the crime scene because of all the trouble the bearded man had gone to. Dinescu could have been killed anywhere, but this particular farm had been chosen. During his visit he had checked the buildings and surrounding areas, but perhaps he was missing something.

Chapter 13
Compromise

Relieved that the threat to his security men appeared to have gone away, Jack Randil flew to Budapest to attend the board meeting at the Hun-Al company. Demeter had already sent him a detailed account of the various problems and the recent stoppage in production due to the use of stolen explosives by the Roma people. Although he had met the Romanian Roma only once, Jack agreed with Demeter that the man was probably co-ordinating the attacks on the mining company. He was impressed with the way the Romanian had persuaded the entire Roma community to move out, which prevented the Hungarian authorities from arresting, or imprisoning them. If the dispute continued, then Jack knew that they faced a clever opponent.

Demeter met him at the airport and as they drove north to his house at Dunakeszi, he gave his friend more details of the succeeding incidents. He was disappointed that he had been unable to find any Roma on his extensive land holding. They agreed that the most sensible action would be to meet with Boldo to try to resolve their differences, but Commissar Radics was in no mood for compromise and would almost certainly make matters worse and provoke more serious attacks. So far no one had been killed, but this would change if they continued to provoke the Roma. The steam engine could have been blown up instead of derailed and the massive digger at the mine could have been destroyed, instead of buried.

Jack saw the attacks on Hun-Al as a campaign of growing resistance to mining company activity with the rail line threatening their village, but intended to send a message.

"Think about it Demeter, it began with a simple derailment, but we kept on building the line towards their village. They steal explosives and we step up security, but still build the line towards their village. They use the explosives on targets, which can be repaired. If we again continue with a line to destroy their village, they could shut down the mine for months. We must persuade Radics to change his attitude."

"You are right Jack, and if we fail to change Radic's attitude, I am going to ask Theresa to postpone her visit and instead, I will try to find the time to fly to the UK."

After changing and eating a meal together, Jack asked if there were any detailed maps of the area and when Demeter had found him a selection, he settled down in the dining room to study them, while his friend worked on his report for the board meeting. An hour later, he asked Demeter if he could borrow the old Kawasaki quad bike he kept in the stables.

"Sure, Jack. I have been using it to look for our missing Roma people and the tank must be at least half full. Be warned though, the seat is splitting and you need to wrap some covering over it to protect your behind. Mine still has scars and I need to get a new seat for it."

After thanking his host, Jack headed for the stables and his tour of the surrounding area. Two hours later, just as dusk was settling in, Demeter was relieved to hear the distinctive sound of the Kawasaki as Jack returned and minutes later, he watched the tall Liverpudlian walking slowly with stiff legs into the room. Although ideal for running up and down the grassy slopes, the vehicle was most uncomfortable and Jack had to sit on the edge of the seat to avoid injury by the exposed springs. After spending time touring the area, Jack now had a picture in his mind so that he was able to get the recent incidents in perspective.

The board meeting was held at an office at the refinery and the tense atmosphere was not helped by the sight and sound of the men working outside to repair the bases and erect the fallen towers. Once they were in position, work would begin to refit the metal chutes and conveyor belt, which would restart feeding ore into the refining process. Demeter made his report, which gave very satisfactory tonnage output prior to the current stoppage. Radics asked if those responsible for the damage had yet been arrested and his face coloured when he heard that no Roma people had been found anywhere in the area. He wanted someone punished for costing the company money through lost profit and repair costs. After a tense silence, Demeter tried to move the meeting forward.

"The area has been thoroughly searched and you have my assurance that there are definitely no Roma in Dunakeszi. They have probably scattered to other Roma communities and we cannot punish people we cannot find. Jack has a proposal I think we should consider."

Jack had a small stack of papers and maps in front of him and began his proposals to the board.

"We have to accept that we have been outsmarted by the local Roma and if we do not reach an agreement with them, I believe they can and will destroy the mine equipment."

Radics slammed his fist on the table as he rose to his feet and interrupted.

"Nonsense. Are we to be held to ransom by a bunch of illiterate Roma? I will bring in troops who will teach these peasants what happens when they interfere with a government operation."

Waiting until the Hungarian had finished speaking and was silently glaring down at him, Jack continued with his proposal.

"However many security staff we bring in, determined men will still find a way to cause damage. As you know, I am ex-military myself and I assure you, saboteurs using small packs of explosives will always have the advantage. We can stop the problems now by moving the track just a half mile from their village."

He handed around maps showing the route, which he had originally planned on one of Demeter's maps and then covered on the quad bike survey. As they studied the maps, he continued with his proposal.

"Smashing our way through their village, which is in a shallow depression, will take us more time than using my route, which runs on flat, clear grassy land."

Radics had listened with a frown on his face and made no effort to study the map Jack had provided and had more to say.

"How do you suggest we speak to these people when we have no idea where they are hiding Mr Randil?"

"We don't need to find them since I am pretty sure they are watching our every move. When we alter the track route to bypass their village, my guess is they will slowly return and we will have no more problems. Our production will soon increase when we have the rail line to move our ore."

Radics shook his head and was obviously not convinced by the Englishman's recommendations.

"So, Mr Randil, we go to all the trouble and extra cost of moving our rail route away from the obvious and direct line in the hope that these missing people will notice and stop disrupting our operations."

"It's either that Commissar, or constant and growing attacks on our installations and a likely end to our export of aluminium ingots and foreign exchange earnings."

There was a strained silence in the room as the two men faced each other and then Dorika Biro spoke. She had remained silent during the argument between the two men, but her voice was firm with authority. She was an experienced mining professional and a government appointee.

"We need the foreign earnings from this mine and we do not need an extended war with people we cannot see. I think the proposal to re-route our rail line is our best option and suggest we put it to a vote."

With one exception, the entire board agreed to change the rail route to avoid the Roma village and wait to see if the attacks then stopped. Commissar Radics was determined to have the last word.

"We will wait to see if Mr Randil's expert knowledge of Roma behaviour is correct. I just hope that we do not go to all the cost and trouble of changing our route for nothing. I can't believe that we are allowing ourselves to be manipulated by these petty criminals."

After the meeting ended, Demeter drove back to his house and congratulated Jack on convincing the board to make a sensible change in policy. Work on preparing the ground for the new route would begin immediately and it was then up to Boldo and his people to reciprocate by causing no more disruption. The giant digger had been put back to work at the mine face and the repairs at the refinery should be finished within days.

"I am so sure that you are right that I will book Theresa into one of the best hotels in Budapest to celebrate."

"That may be fine for you and the love of your life Demeter, but what do I get for saving your mine, provided that I am right of course?"

"I will continue to tell everyone how smart you are and that I am lucky to have such a good friend."

Nodding his head towards his companion Jack told him that he should wait to see if he was right first. After waiting for three days, he was ready to fly back to England. During that time, some of the Roma had returned to their village. His guess had been right, but what next? The Roma problem might now have been solved, but he had not really identified the people behind the attacks on his security men in Liverpool, or their intentions. Since the Roma people would not now have to relocate, there would not be a demand for cash, or help to compensate them for a forced move from their homes. Hoping that the problems in the Hun-Al operation were now resolved, he must concentrate his attention on the major threat to his business in Liverpool.

Chapter 14
Executions

Kirill rented a small building on a run-down industrial estate at Sefton Park, which was within easy access of the city centre. It had previously been used by a small engineering company, Cummings Bros, which had gone into bankruptcy. After making a deal with the owners, he took over the fitted workshop, two small furnished offices and a reception area. There were steel roller shutter doors in a side entrance and a small door at the front into a vestibule with a counter to deal with customers.

He bought a used white Ford Transit van, which would not look out of place on the estate and would provide concealment for those inside. The van would be used to pick up his men, so that it would be the only vehicle seen entering the building and create minimum interest. Its comings and goings, if noticed at all, would be seen as making deliveries, or providing service. As an added cover, he had the previous company name and a false telephone number painted on the sides of the van.

After keeping a close watch on two members of the Young Guns he blamed for killing Ahtoh, he had gathered a record of their regular movements and could predict where they were likely to be on a particular day and time. Tim Branton was in his mid-thirties, roughly six feet in height and had a muscular frame. Darrel Williams was slightly shorter and older, but with broad shoulders. Both kept themselves fit by working out in the evenings at Joe Devine's gymnasium. It was Wednesday evening and the BMW 525 saloon drove into the car park, and the two Young Guns walked to the Devine Fitness Studio for their usual two-hour workout. Ten minutes later, a small blue van drove up and parked alongside the BMW. The two men inside remained in their seats as they waited for the Young Guns to complete their training session and return to the BMW.

Eventually, the two men walked through the studio entrance with their sports bags slung over their shoulders. Busy in conversation, they took no notice of the two men standing near the opened rear door of the blue van. Tim stopped near the driver's side and was opening the door when he felt a pain in his head and then collapsed into the arms of his attacker. Darrel sensed that something was wrong and turned to help his friend before being clubbed down himself. Both unconscious men were quickly lifted into the rear of the van and tied up before it drove off. The BMW remote fob lay on the ground alongside the unlocked car, together with two sports bags.

Jack Randil had returned from his Hun-Al meeting in Hungary the previous day and was having coffee with Joe Devine when the two Young Guns passed their table after finishing their training. The two pairs nodded to each other, but did not speak.

Jack was giving Joe an account of the problems in Hungary and after finishing his coffee, glanced through the window and was surprised to see the BMW still in the car park.

"That's strange Joe, it must be at least ten minutes since Branton and Williams walked out, but their BMW is still there."

Joe turned to look through the window and around the car park.

"They usually drive straight off and there is no sign of them in the car park. Is that a bag on the ground near the car?"

Rising to his feet Jack walked out to check on the car and was followed by Joe. Finding the remote fob and bags beside an unlocked and empty car made it very likely that the gang members had been kidnapped. Jack rang the city police with full details of the likely abduction and the two men returned to the café area to wait for the arrival of the police. They were drinking more coffee when Inspector Peter Kilshaw arrived after joining the team sent to investigate.

"What is your take on this Jack?"

"My guess is that we are about to see the start of the next stage of Russian Mafia entry into the city crime world and we had better be prepared for some very nasty activity."

"I hope you are wrong Jack, but abducting two tough gang members in daylight and full view of Joe's place is bold and professional and it looks as if you are right. We could all be dragged into this."

The evening edition of the *Liverpool Echo* gave details of the two missing men and the abandoned car, but at the request of the police, did not make any mention of a possible link with Russian Mafia. Geraint Davies was the same reporter who had written about Jack Randil's letter to customers and he had immediately made the connection. Two days later, a small parcel was delivered to him personally at the paper. After removing the outer wrappings, he found a shoebox and instead of removing the lid, decided to contact the police.

Past warnings about shoebox bombs had flashed through his head and he decided that even if it was a hoax, he preferred to look a fool rather than risk being maimed. He had co-operated with the police over his description of the abandoned BMW and missing men and the box was taken to a safe area. It was opened by trained staff wearing protective clothing. The sight of a human hand and a penis covered in congealed blood, together with two gold rings and two expensive watches was such a shock, that even hardened police staff were affected. Geraint Davies was violently sick as he staggered away from the steel table on which the box had been opened.

After spending time in the toilet and cleaning himself up, Geraint re-joined the small group of policemen meeting in an adjoining room.

The general view was that the body parts had come from the two missing Young Guns men. Laboratory tests would show whether the parts were removed before, or after death. DNA tests should prove their identities, but the watches and rings had been included to show this and emphasise that the expensive jewellery was insignificant. The killers wanted to send a message and a warning. The abductions and the shoebox contents were a declaration of war.

After the identities had been proven, the families of the two men would be informed and together with the forensic reports, they might have some idea on how they had died. Geraint was asked to avoid mention of the shoebox issue until the police received the essential information. He would then be given clearance to print some of the facts. If the Russian Mafia was responsible, then by sending the gruesome remains to him, they would have expected him to go to print. The deaths and amputations would scare both members of the Young Guns and the general population. Inspector Kershaw thanked Geraint for his co-operation and as they were both friends of Jack Randil, he trusted the man to remain silent on the double atrocities.

Kirill was pleased that his planning was working out so well. The two men had been attacked and brought to the Sefton Park unit without a hitch. The van stolen the same morning for the abduction was driven to a deserted rubbish tip, doused with petrol and then set on fire. Both men were taken into the workshop, stripped and then tightly bound and gagged. Tim Branton was the first to regain consciousness and he was told that he would be expected to give Kirill full details of the Young Guns operation if he wanted to stay alive. He shook his head and was obviously determined to give them no information.

When Darrel was awake, the two men were laid side by side on a wide workbench covered by a heavy plastic sheet, with an industrial drill suspended over their heads. Both were asked if they were willing to provide the necessary information and both shook their heads. The drill was moved above their bodies and came to rest just inches above Tim's knee. Once again, he was asked about giving the information on his gang's activities and membership and again, he shook his head. The drill was switched on and slowly lowered. His screams were muffled by the gag in his mouth, but his body writhed with the pain.

Darrel was asked if he was ready to talk about the gang's operations and he immediately nodded his head. His gag was removed and Kirill began asking about the names and addresses of gang members, their customers and operations, as well as the location of their records and bank details. Kirill then attached a clamp to Darrel's penis before asking many of the same questions again to be sure that the previous answers were accurate. Finally, he was asked about the brawl in the Tropicana Bistro and the gang's attack on Ahtoh. He claimed that he had not been in the Bistro that particular night.

Shaking his head, Kirill replaced Darrel's gag and slowly turned the tightening screw, Darrel's body arched with the pain, but he was tightly bound and could only make moaning noises as his head turned from side to side. Looking down at both men, Kirill told them his intentions.

72

"You both showed no mercy to my countryman when you beat him to death on the street of your city and I will show you none. You, Tim, are a man and will die quickly. Darrel is a coward and a liar and since I know he was at the Tropicana with the mob who killed Ahtoh, we will make him pay by removing his manhood."

Kirill nodded to one of his men and Tim was stabbed through the heart and then the man used a pair of metal cutters to remove Darrel's penis. They took a coffee break and sat around a desk while their victim bled out and placed a pile of old wadding alongside to absorb the blood. Kiril did not want any overflowing onto the floor as evidence of a crime. The same cutters were used to cut off Tim's right hand. The bloodied body parts were put into a shoebox together with watches and rings removed from the bodies. Kirill had kept a copy of the *Liverpool Echo* with the article by the reporter with the strange name, who had written about a likely Russian Mafia presence in the city. The box was wrapped and addressed to him personally at the paper.

There was a furnace in the workshop. The two bodies were cut into small sections and then wrapped in the blood-soaked plastic sheet with their clothing, before being sprinkled with creosote. After midnight, when the industrial area was mainly deserted, the bodies would be incinerated. The creosote had been added to help minimise the distinctive stench of burning flesh. Kirill wanted no evidence of the killings to remain in his new haven. His men were all wearing blue boiler suits and heavy working boots, so that any watchers would see only engineers getting on with their work. The patch pockets were useful for them to carry their guns and knives without looking suspicious.

The information from Darrel would help them to plan their attack on the Young Guns and discourage any of the other gangs from interfering with the new criminal leaders in the city. Their first move would be to visit the banker who looked after the Young Guns funds.

Chapter 15
Intrusion

Demeter had been convinced that there would be a running battle between the mineworkers and the Roma. Fortunately, with Jack's help, the Roma threat to the Hun-Al mine had been removed. Anxious to begin restoring relations with the Roma, he drove to the village with two of the armed security men to meet some of those who had already returned. Five of the previously abandoned homes now had families living in them. He reassured those he met that the railway line to the mine would not now be built through the middle of their community and they were relieved to hear that their homes were safe.

Jack had anticipated that a watch would be kept on company actions and news about the change in route of the railway line would be noticed and acted upon. Demeter hoped that everything would soon be restored to normal and asked the Roma who returned to tell Boldo that he would like to meet him and arrange work at the mine for those who wanted it.

At the refinery both towers had been replaced and work on the linking chutes and conveyor belts would soon be finished, so that the refining process could be restarted. The mine was already in full production and without further disruptions, the rail link between the mine and the refinery should begin moving raw ore within three weeks. The route lay over relatively flat land, apart from one small stream in a narrow depression, where a separate team of men were already building a short steel and concrete crossing. With everything apparently operating to plan and peace restored in the area, Demeter looked forward to meeting his fiancée Theresa in Budapest over the coming weekend.

Jack Randil as Chairman of the Liverpool Trades Council had returned from Hungary in good time to prepare for his meeting in Frankfurt with their German opposite numbers. Regular meetings were held to improve cross trading between the two cities and Jack was able to use his fluency in German to translate for those members unable to speak the other's language. After the Trades Council meeting was finished, Jack met up with current and prospective customers to negotiate deliveries of aluminium ingots from the Hungarian Hun-Al operation. When he returned from Germany, he heard about the delivery of the shoebox with the dismembered parts of two of the Young Guns gang.

He was at the Leisure Centre after his squash game with Peter Kershaw and as usual was joined in their after-game drink in the bar by his brother in law, Greg Ridd. The policeman described the delivery and contents of the box and admitted that he and his police colleagues were shocked. They had seen many forms of crime in the city, but the sheer barbarism of the act reached new levels. The three men agreed that although they had passed on a warning about the foreign criminal threat, the two members of the Young Guns could not have expected, or protected themselves from their well-planned abduction and subsequent murder.

Jack was quick to sum up the likely outcome.

"We can now expect a war in the city with casualties on both sides. If the Young Guns can stop the spread of the Russians, things will not be too different, since they have never bothered us. If the Russians win, then we can expect our security men to be the next targets. Many have already been in combat, but they have families and I would not expect them to risk their lives to protect buildings and customer equipment."

Peter agreed and told them that the Russians had obviously wanted to shock and frighten people in Liverpool by having details of the shoebox contents featured in the *Liverpool Echo*. Instead, the newspaper simply stated that it had received a delivery of personal items, identified as belonging to the missing men and that the police were now looking for those responsible for the murders.

"I agree Jack that it would be better for us all if the Young Guns can stop them, but they are all criminals and the police must be impartial and simply apply the law."

As the three men drank their beer and discussed the impending battle, two men stood outside the front door of a detached house in a quiet avenue in Aigburth on the south side of the city. When a woman answered their knock and opened the door, they forced her back inside and pushed past her into the entrance hall of the house. A portly, middle-aged man wearing slippers shuffled into the hall to see who was visiting him in the evening and was struck in the face and knocked down. One man dragged the woman into the lounge, while the other grabbed the fallen householder by the collar of his cardigan and lifted him off his feet, before carrying him into the room and dumping him in a chair.

An eighteen-year-old girl was curled up on the sofa with head phones plugged in as she listened to music from her Walkman music player. Seeing her father stretched out in a chair next to her she tried to scream, but a large hand covered her mouth and nose and a knife blade was held in front of her face. Working quickly and efficiently, the two men bound and gagged all three and then waited for Gary Dempsey to regain consciousness. When Gary opened his eyes, he saw his wife and daughter with two men beside them holding large knives. His eyes registered shock and fear as he guessed that these must be the men involved in the murder of his two friends.

One of the intruders was obviously the leader and did all the talking, but Gary was surprised that both were dressed in blue overalls and looked like plumbers, or manual workers.

"You are Dempsey and you are the bank man for your friends, these Young Guns, yes?"

Gary shook his head and the man motioned to his colleague, who quickly tore and cut away all the young girl's clothes and then tied her to a chair. She sat with her knees pressed tightly together, head down so that her long auburn hair hung over her face as tears streamed from her eyes in shame. She had well-formed breasts and after fondling them, the man lightly traced the point of his knife under each so that it just broke the skin and left a red outline. The leader spoke again.

"Your daughter is pretty girl and you not want her to be cut up by my friend with his knife. Afterwards, I do the same to your woman. Better that you help us and then we go and leave you and your family with your eyes and lips and ears, yes."

Gary was horrified as he watched the big man standing alongside his naked daughter Rosanne, with his knife blade resting on her bare breast. He had to save her and nodded his head vigorously to show he would help them. His gag was removed and he told them where he kept the bank details. The leader Gregor already knew a great deal about how the money was collected and brought to Gary, so that he could maintain five separate accounts with local banks to cover expenses. The bulk of the takings from the various activities were forwarded to an offshore account through a number of illegal and untraceable operations.

Once he had given the account numbers and passwords, the details were telephoned through to Kirill at Sefton Park. After switching off his phone, the smiling man in blue overalls asked Gary when the next cash delivery would be made by one of the gang leaders. He nodded his head when he learned that a delivery was expected during the evening, since this matched the details already given by Darrel. Gary was gagged again and all three family members were tied to chairs. The house telephone rang and thinking it might be a message about the expected cash delivery, Gregor removed the gag from Gary and warned him what would happen if he betrayed them. He then cradled the phone between them so that when he answered, they could both listen.

"Hi Mac, is Danny there?"

Gregor shook his head and indicated that Gary should answer the caller. Gary spoke carefully into the phone with the Russian holding a knife near his throat.

"No, there are no Danny's here, sorry wrong number."

Gregor nodded his head in satisfaction and replaced the gag in Gary's mouth. The intruders made themselves tea in the kitchen as they waited for their next victim to arrive. When the glare of a car's headlights lit the hall, the Russians positioned themselves just inside the front door and Gregor gripped his knife in his right hand. When the doorbell rang, he wrenched open the door with his left hand and thrust the knife forward to stab the visitor, but the man was standing over to the side and the knife only grazed his left arm.

Standing in the full beam of the car headlights, Gregor was a perfect target and Don Taylor, aiming through the open car window shot him twice in the chest and Gregor toppled backwards before collapsing on the floor. His companion rushed into the doorway with his automatic pistol raised, but was immediately struck by two bullets from a Young Gun standing guard outside. The bodies of both Russians lay alongside each other on the floor and were left in their own blood as the wounded man had his knife wound bound. The noise of the gunfire alarmed neighbours and was reported three times to the police, who sent armed men to investigate.

At Sefton Park, Kirill had yet to learn of the death of two of his men and was busy trying to send details of the Young Guns offshore bank account to his superiors. After the dismembered body parts of their colleagues had been sent to the newspaper, the Young Guns leader Don Taylor had expected that torture would probably be used to obtain details of their operations. Changes were quickly made and extra security was added in vulnerable areas. The phone call was a security check and if all was safe, the answer should have been that Danny was there. Gary had told them there was more than one intruder by saying there were no Dannys. Don Taylor decided to lead his men and show that he knew how to deal with foreign interlopers. After the vicious killing of their friends, they showed no mercy.

Gary Dempsey knew that help would soon arrive and when giving Gregor details of the offshore account number, he deliberately transposed a five and an eight number to prevent the money being stolen.

Kirill had unwisely underestimated his opponents and his men had paid the price. With four of his team already arrested and a total of three killed, his superiors would not be pleased. Gregor had been one of his English speakers and his second in command and would be difficult to replace, even if he was able to persuade his leaders to send reinforcements. When he discovered how his men had been ambushed, he would know that his future career and life were both under threat.

Don Taylor quickly briefed Gary Dempsey and his wife on the story they would give the police, before he and his men left the scene. Gary then called the police to report the attack on his family and killings on his doorstep by an unknown assassin. The armed police arrived first and called in the crime scene team. Inspector Peter Kershaw walked around the staff working in the doorway and checking the two bodies. After hearing that both men had been shot twice in the chest, he spoke to Gary in his lounge. The daughter had now dressed and sat in a chair and sobbed as her father described what had happened. Peter went over the statement to be sure he had full details.

"So you were all tied up and gagged and you knew these men were somewhere in your house, but were unable to see them. Then you heard the sound of guns fired and your wife was able to loosen your hands so that you could use the phone to call 999."

"Yes, that's what happened, inspector."

"Is this what you remembered happened, Mrs Dempsey."

The woman nodded her head, but was still in shock and unable to speak. Peter realised that he would have to concentrate his interrogation on the man, who seemed eager to cooperate, but Peter suspected that he was unlikely to be told the whole truth.

"After you were all tied up, how long was it before you heard the shooting?"

"I couldn't see my watch, or the clock, but it must have been at least half an hour."

"Why do you think you were attacked and tied up?"

"I am a respectable accountant in the city and I can only assume that it was a case of mistaken identity, which is probably why they didn't harm us, apart from hitting me when they broke in."

"Have you checked to see if anything has been taken?"

"I have only had time to have a quick walk through the rooms, but our valuables are locked in the safe and it has not been tampered with."

Peter knew that Gary was lying and was connected with the Young Guns, but the men had been shot from outside the house and he couldn't see Gary as having the courage, or the skill to put two bullets into the chest of each of them. It had to be part of the battle between the two gangs, but this time the Young Guns had come out on top. Both dead men were wearing working overalls and he wondered if the disguise was intended to help them to gain entry to the house. The men were probably Russians and so far, the struggle for control of Liverpool had cost the lives of five men. He wondered how many more would die before it was settled.

Two guns had been found and neither had been fired, which suggested an assassination rather than confrontation. The guns were Makarov automatics firing 9 mm bullets, which were probably Russian made. The men also carried military style knives with six-inch blades, which Peter recognised through his own Marine Commando background as Kizlyar, frequently used by Russian special forces.

The Russians must have wanted something from the Dempsey home, either cash, or information. Once the two bodies had been removed for the post mortem, he would check what they were carrying to see if there was any clue to their presence at the house. Once again there would be nothing to identify them.

Chapter 16
Investigation

Lieutenant Bumbesco drove to the isolated farm with two constables, still trying to clear the nagging doubt in his mind that he had missed something on his previous visit. The farmer Butaco opened his door and was surprised to receive yet another visit from the police. He invited his visitors in for coffee and Bumbesco began asking his questions.

"This bearded man who overpowered you arrived early when you had just eaten your breakfast. Roughly how long was it before he released you?"

"I was tied up in my own cellar for almost the whole day, since it was the middle of the afternoon when I heard him drive away. I came up to the kitchen and looked through my window to make sure he had gone."

"You heard a car drive away, but did you also hear a car arrive earlier in the day?"

"Yes. The engine was very noisy and I heard it come after I had been in the cellar for three, or four hours and my back was giving me hell from lying on the floor down there."

Bumbesco nodded his head and thought that the farmer's attacker certainly had plenty of time for whatever he wanted to do. His guess was right and there had to be a reason why this particular farm had been chosen. So what had the bearded man been doing that took him four hours. It had to be something in preparation for Dinescu's arrival.

"Your visitor must have been doing something in all that time. Did you see anything different when you looked around the house and your land?"

"No, nothing really, except that he must have wanted some exercise, because he dug that area behind my barn. I thought I might as well use it to plant some old potatoes. He also went off with an old door that I used to stack boxes."

If the stranger had been digging, it was probably to hide something, or he suddenly thought, to bury something. When he coupled his last thought with the missing door, he began to realise the likely horror of what had been done.

"Do you have any long steel rods we could use?"

"Yes, I have some which I use to hang bird scarers near my crops."

He asked his two policemen to begin prodding the newly dug area with the long rods, starting from the side near the hard top soil, which had not been dug over. Each policeman would cover a band roughly a metre wide. He reasoned that the man would not want to carry a heavy object too far over the soft soil and began nearest the farmhouse. Halfway down the first band, the steel rod hit a solid object, which seemed to be a metre wide. The soil was cleared away and an old door was exposed. When this was lifted, the policemen were horrified to look down on the contorted dead body of the missing soldier.

There were no signs of injury from their cursory examination and Bumbesco was sure that the murderer had once again made his victim suffer, by burying him alive. He tried to prevent his mind from imagining the desperation and agonies that the soldier had suffered and made a vow that he would do everything possible to catch the monster responsible. He telephoned through to his office to arrange for staff to come and examine the area and take the body away for the post mortem.

A full report was sent to Police HQ at Bucharest and copied to the army barracks where Dinescu had been stationed. At the end of his report on the murder of Dinescu, an appraisal had been added by Bumbesco. He outlined his suspicions that the deaths of Commissar Dalca and Dinescu were linked. He suggested that the destruction of Budestin, the Roma village where a soldier was stabbed and a young boy and old woman shot was the motive. He was convinced that the murders were in revenge for the shooting of the boy and old woman. It also seemed likely that another soldier, the man, Gunari, sent to investigate the earlier crucifixion of a Hungarian, had also been killed at Budestin.

A week later, Bumbesco was at a meeting at Bucharest with the colonel in charge of his division, the major who was his commanding officer and an army major from Dinescu's barracks. He had convinced the others that the man most likely to be responsible was Tigo, the leader of the tribe who was absent during both visits by the soldiers. Bumbesco had recently interviewed the soldier struck by a slingshot on the first visit, who was also present when the village was burned. He stated that the old woman who was shot was Tigo's mother and the man had a reputation for violence and as a tyrant.

At this point the colonel could contain his anger no longer.

"We believed that someone who suffered when Dalca was working for the old regime had killed him, but we will not tolerate the Tigani torturing and killing a senior government official, as well as two of our soldiers. I want this man caught and punished and you have my full support with whatever you need to do it."

"Thank you, sir. I would like to offer a reward for information leading to Tigo's capture and have temporary leave to work in the Budestin area. If we can locate posters in the Tigani villages spread around there, we may tempt someone who has been beaten by Tigo to make contact and help us. I would also like an assistant, either from the police, or army, who has a Tigani background. He should be able to work in the area to find some of those who have left Budestin, but know what happened to our man Gunari. We all know that there is very little chance that the Tigani will talk to our own policemen, or soldiers."

"Very good Bumbesco, you have my full support and your Major Chisca will make all the necessary arrangements. I hope you will find this Tigo, but be careful that he does not kill you too, or another of our Tigani volunteers."

The meeting ended and the colonel left, but the others remained to work together on the details of the search for Tigo in Călăraşi County, where Budestin was located. Major Chisca had already been told that a Tigani would be needed to ferret out the information Bumbesco wanted and had two policemen in mind. He would arrange for interviews to choose the best man for the job. The reward offered would be set at 50,000,000 Leu, which should be very tempting to poor Tigani.

"I would like to start as soon as possible, if I may, sir. When can I interview the two Tigani policemen?"

Major Chisca told him that they worked near Bucharest and he could see them both tomorrow afternoon.

Bumbesco was amazed that all his suggestions had been accepted and that he would soon begin his hunt for the monster who had killed so ruthlessly. The following afternoon, he visited Police HQ to interview the Tigani policemen. The first man was nervous and seemed concerned about working out in the countryside on his own. The second was a big, chubby and lively candidate who seemed willing to tackle anything. He was also a martial arts fanatic and should be able to defend himself if he was attacked. His name was Rudari and his parents had taught him to speak the Romani language, as well as his normal Romanian. Bumbesco took an instant liking to the man and chose him for the walkabout in Călăraşi County. He gave Rudari, who asked to be called Rudi, full details of the murders and explained the search for the killer Tigo. Rudi was married with two children and although told about the possible danger in finding and arresting Tigo, the bearded Tigani was still keen to get involved. He was shocked to learn about the cruelty of the two killings and wanted Tigo to pay for his crimes.

Bumbesco arranged the placement of the reward notices with Major Chisca in villages where they would travel. Rudi agreed to begin his search in two days, after he had made sure his family would be cared for by nearby relatives while he was absent. Rudi's family owned a Tigani wagon, or vardo, with tall wheels and a canvas roof hung on metal hoops. It was made from spruce wood for lightness and was at least fifty years old and drawn by one horse and he would use it for his journey through the area. Bumbesco would cover the same area, but avoid visiting the actual Tigani communities and instead arrange to meet Rudi at intervals for updates.

The search area would start around Bacău and the vardo was taken by lorry to the nearby town of Focşani for Rudi to begin moving north.

Bumbesco needed to keep in touch with Rudi and he carried a mobile phone and arranged to make a hunting trip in the area to be near at hand if Rudi found Tigo. Rudi would then find a public phone to contact him. They decided it was unsafe for Rudi to carry a mobile phone and risk having it found, since they were rarely used by Roma travellers. Bumbesco had often hunted with his father and with the wild life in the densely forested region, he should not raise suspicions if he travelled as a hunter and drove his father's Suzuki off-roader. Experienced in the danger from brown bears, he packed a pepper spray as well as his hunting rifle and knife and also carried a small automatic pistol. Well aware of the brown bear's incredible ability to smell food from a distance before making their way to the source, he packed mainly salad food and would start the day with a big breakfast and have dinner at his overnight location. It would be dangerous to stay overnight in the forest. He made sure that he had a good supply of drinking water to avoid dehydration in the hot sun.

Although he believed that Tigo would return to his own people, the man could have moved far away. However, since he had taken care to hide his identity and cover his tracks when carrying out the murders, he would assume he was safe. Bumbesco hoped that the search in the area would show results within two weeks, but knew that at most he could expect to continue the search for only four, or five weeks. After this, another meeting would be held to decide on further action.

Chapter 17
Extinction

Kirill had heard nothing from Gregor after the offshore bank account details were given to him over the phone and he had then transferred the information to his Moscow contact. The two men should have returned some time ago with yet another Young Guns member. He knew it would be dangerous to drive to the accountants' house and unwise to ring Gregor. If they had walked into a trap, there was little he could do and he knew from his own treatment of the Young Guns captives that men can be made to talk.

As he was considering possible mishaps to his men, he received a terse message from his Moscow contacts. Despite three attempts to access the Young Guns account in the offshore bank, they had been unable to do so and told Kirill that his account number was false. It was another failure in his leadership and somehow the moneyman Dempsey had outwitted Gregor and risked his own and his family's lives to protect the Young Guns bank account. Thinking over possibilities, he decided that it could have been an unlucky break and Gregor had run into a group of Young Guns, or his own attack had been anticipated and countered.

If he could still obtain the offshore account details and punish this man Dempsey at the same time, he would send the right messages to Moscow and the Young Guns. He knew that their leader was called Taylor and he needed to test how clever and resourceful the man was. He guessed that Dempsey would be careful and would probably be protected, but there was a young daughter who could be an easier target and bring Dempsey to him. He planned two separate attacks on his foes. The first was intended to distract them while he launched his main action.

Les Perrin took the phone call as he sat in his car in the car park off Victoria Street. One of his regular customers was waiting at the bottom of Water Street and Les drove down and picked him up. Money was exchanged for drugs and the satisfied customer was dropped off in Pall Mall and Les returned to his stand off Victoria Street. He was kept busy and when his stock was almost cleared, he made a phone call to have more brought to him. A motor cycle roared into the car park and stopped alongside Les' car. The rider opened his side pannier to pass a package to Les. A dark figure suddenly appeared from behind the car and another from the front. The motor cyclist had his throat cut and Les was stabbed in the throat through the open car window.

A driver returning to his car parked alongside found the overturned motor cycle and body and hearing a car engine running, looked into the car and saw yet another body. He called the police and was soon surrounded by flashing blue lights as another crime scene was investigated. Both men were known to be active in the drug trade and employed by the Young Guns. No cash or drugs were found and Peter Kershaw suspected that although it looked like a robbery, it was more likely to be another attack by the Russian Mafia. The battle for supremacy between the two gangs was raising the city murder rate to record levels and as yet he had found no information on the numbers, or possible location of the foreign criminals.

Don Taylor was protecting Gary Dempsey as he drove to and from his office and he was watched in his home, because Don expected the Russians to punish him for his part in the death of their colleagues. Unfortunately, he could not protect the dozens of dealers and members of his drug supply chain. Les Perrin had brought in a lot of money and he guessed the attacks had only just begun. He had offered a big reward for any information on the Russians and if he found them, they would be dead. They were probably set up within the city boundary and using a detached house with ample grounds, or an industrial building where their movement would not be noticed, nor any unusual noise from their torture and killing of captured colleagues.

Rosanne Dempsey was furious that her father would not allow her to go out in the evenings because of the men who had been killed at their house. She did not know that he was deeply involved with a criminal gang and had believed his explanation to the policeman that it was a case of mistaken identity. He was at a meeting tonight and she was nineteen years old and had to stay indoors whilst her friends went to a disco. She locked her bedroom door, put on some music and climbed out of her bedroom window onto the flat roof of the garage to step down on a water butt to reach the ground. She left by the garden gate and walked quickly down the road, passing one of Kirill's watchers as she went.

The disco was hot, crowded and very noisy, and Rosanne was cooling off with a drink when one of the club employees approached her to tell her that her father was in hospital and her mother had sent a taxi to collect her. With guilt uppermost in her mind after disobeying her father's request, she rushed to the club entrance and saw a taxi with a man alongside holding the door open for her. She jumped into the back, the door was closed and the taxi drove off. She knew Liverpool well and should have noticed that they were driving in the wrong direction. By the time she began to have worries about the route they were taking, they had almost reached the industrial area in Sefton Park where Kirill was waiting for her. The taxi stopped and a man opened the door and pulled her out of her seat. The stolen taxi was then driven away and abandoned in a side street.

Gary Dempsey returned home from his meeting, accompanied by his bodyguard and was told Rosanne was listening to music in her room. He was unhappy about having to restrict her movements and walked upstairs to speak to her. After knocking twice, he tried her door and was surprised that it was locked. He could hear the music and knocked much harder, with no response. Beginning to panic, he went to fetch a spare key and entered the bedroom. The window was open and Rosanne was not in her room. Guessing that she had gone to the disco he had told her not to visit, he began ringing her friends. They told him about the hospital message and the waiting taxi and his heart sank as he guessed who had taken her. He thought about calling Don Taylor, but knew the man would rather save his money than Rosanne.

His wife was distraught and blamed him for being involved with crooks and risking their lives. As he tried to console her, his phone rang and he was given instructions on what he should do to save his daughter. He was warned that if he contacted the police, he would never see his daughter again. Kirill wanted the full and accurate account numbers and when money had been taken from the offshore accounts, Rosanne would be freed unharmed. Gary had a difficult choice to make. If he gave the Russians the information they wanted, he would save Rosanne, but Don Taylor would certainly kill him. If he did not, Rosanne would be killed. He suddenly remembered the Liverpool city councillor who had exposed local corruption and helped the people in Seaforth to save their houses from demolition. The man also owned a large business, which provided security cover throughout the city.

Jack Randil was finishing off his beer with Peter Kershaw after their weekly squash game when his phone rang and an emotional Gary Dempsey told him about his daughter's abduction. The two had spoken previously at business functions in the city, but Jack had not been aware of his connection with the Young Guns.

"I'm sorry to hear about your daughter Gary, and I will do all I can to help, but let me give this some thought first and I will ring you back."

Peter guessed what the conversation was about from Jack's questions and the overheard comments of the high-pitched voice of Dempsey. Jack explained the situation and the threat to kill the young girl if police were involved, as well as the likelihood of Dempsey being killed by Don Taylor. Dempsey had been told that he would be contacted again by phone and that he must have the information ready. Jack had a possible plan forming in his mind.

"If you can keep this quiet, I will suggest to Gary that he tells the Russians that he wants his daughter saved at all costs and to make sure there are no slipups, he will meet them and arrange the computer transfer himself. Can we put a small bug on him and then follow him to their hideout so that we save the girl and get the Russians? It will need an armed team of police because we know they are armed. As the Russians are watching Gary set up the computer transfer, your men will have to break in and use stun grenades, or tear gas to confuse them before they can kill Dempsey and his daughter. It will still be a high-risk situation, but at least the poor man will have an even chance to save his own and his daughter's life and we get the Russians, whatever happens."

"I knew Dempsey was lying about being attacked because of mistaken identity. The Russians were after the account details all along and got jumped by the Young Guns. It sounds possible Jack, but do you think Gary can convince them to let him go to them and what if the building they are using has no windows, which we need for the stun grenades?"

"I think it best to let Gary decide if he wants to take his chances Peter, since his alternatives are pretty grim."

"This could back fire on us Jack, and end up with both Gary and Rosanne killed, but you are right, we would get the Russians and stop the war raging in the city. Rosanne's chances of being released are also pretty slim, since I expect she has seen their faces and killing her is safer for them. I will have to clear this with my super."

"Right, Peter. You ring your super and I will put it to Gary and let him decide."

Gary listened as he was told about the plan and was silent for some time at the other end of the phone. As an accountant he was used to balancing facts and figures, but this time his judgement involved lives. He made his choice.

"I will try to talk them into letting me make the transfer and hope you can kill them all and end this. I know I have no chance at all if I trade the account details for Rosanne and then have to rely on their promise to let her go."

Peter had made his call to his super who agreed to Jack's proposal and suggested that Jack should visit Gary at his home to tape the small transmitter in his shoe and go over his intended offer to the Russians. Since the two men knew each other, his visit would be less suspicious if the house was watched. The police also planned to use their helicopter to shadow whatever vehicle the transmitter was moving in. Two armed police teams would be waiting at separate locations in case of unexpected mishaps. The transmitter would be delivered to Jack's home later that night and he would call on Gary at 9 am the following morning, when the police would be ready to follow him. When Gary was told, he suggested that Jack should carry a briefcase to make it look as if it was calling on business.

A policewoman came to his home with the tracking device and showed Jack how it operated. Judy was not at all happy that once again her husband was involving himself in dangerous affairs and he had to reassure her that it was only a minor role. The following morning, Jack called at the Dempsey home and fitted the transmitter. For the next twenty minutes, they discussed how Gary would respond when the Russians contacted him and then Jack left to drive to his office. As soon as Gary left the house, the police would know and begin to track him. The telephone call came at 10 am and as he pleaded with Kirill to let him make the transfer, the Russian decided that having Gary make the transfer would guarantee that the money would be accessed this time. It could well be his last chance to restore his reputation with his leaders and he dare not risk another failure. After the money transfer, he would kill Dempsey and his daughter.

Kirill was familiar with the city centre and chose Lime Street station as the safest meeting point. It would be busy and there were a number of exits to choose from. Gary was to wait near the Skelhorn Street exit at 11 am until he was contacted. His man would first check that Gary was alone and that there were no watchers and then lead him through the station, with another Russian checking that they were not followed. The waiting van would be in a side street and Kirill would be driving.

When told about Gary's instructions, Superintendent Larry James decided it could jeopardise the operation to have men at the station and instead they would rely on the transmitter and helicopter. Gary was tracked up London Road and on to Brownlow Hill before stopping at a Sefton Park location. The two police vans moved towards the address using flashing lights, but with no sirens, which might alert the Russians. A car pulled out in front of one van and caused a minor collision. The stubborn driver would not move his car until he was threatened with arrest for obstruction and failing to give way to the police van.

The second police van drove into the small industrial estate and stopped near the Cummings Bros building, but could see no sign of the Cummings van. A call to the helicopter brought the report that it had driven inside the building. Knowing that they must gain access quickly, the policemen first blocked the roller shutter entrance with their van and then hurried to the windows. They were frustrated to find the windows too high and small to allow access without risking their lives. They decided instead to aim and if necessary, fire through the windows. One policeman saw a stack of wooden pallets near the building and as they were using them to build vantage platforms, the second police van arrived.

With a full group, two platforms were soon built. One policeman then climbed the stack and smashed the window, whilst his colleague threw in a stun grenade. Kirill was standing behind Gary, who was seated at a computer and taking as long as possible to enter the codes as he waited for the police to save him. Suddenly, one of the windows was smashed and as he cowered beside the computer table, he heard a loud bang. He found himself totally disoriented. One Russian was standing near the window and he quickly turned and aimed his gun at the helmeted figure looking down at him from outside. Before he could fire, he was shot through the head. Kirill had fallen to the floor, but although dazed he was still holding his gun and shot Gary in the back. The policeman watching at the window then shot Kirill.

Another pair of policemen smashed their way into the reception area and entered with guns at the ready. Hearing the noise, the Russians guarding Rosanne rushed from the room and with guns in their hands were shot as they ran through the door into reception. The Russians were all armed and with their reputation for violence, the guns in their hands brought their instant deaths.

After checking the building and finding that all four Russians were dead, an ambulance was summoned and Gary and Rosanne were taken away. The bullet had struck him in the shoulder and although it was a nasty wound, he should soon recover. He had told Jack in the morning that if he survived the day, he would end his connection with criminals, since his family was more important to him than the money. He had twice risked his life to protect Don Taylor's offshore account and hoped he had earned his release from the gang. During the evening, Gary was visited in his hospital bed by Don Taylor, who thanked him for protecting the offshore bank deposits. When Gary told him that he wanted to end his connection with the gang, he was told that it was a lifetime position for as long as he and his family were alive. The comment left Gary depressed and ashamed that his family was also bound to this man.

When Jack was given details of the successful rescue, he was finally able to relax after worrying that his idea might lead to the deaths of the young girl and her father. Superintendent James was very pleased with the outcome and rang to thank him for his help. The big surprise came the next day when an enormous bunch of flowers was delivered to Jack's home, addressed to Mrs Judy Randil. The accompanying card simply said, "Thanks, Don Taylor." Jack was not anxious to mix with a local gang, but they had never interfered in his business and an ally is better than an enemy. Discussing the change in policy with Greg when the Russians stopped their attacks on Randil Security, he thought they had been lucky.

"If that big Russian had not got drunk in the city centre bar, our men would certainly have suffered. The Russians were upset when one of their own was beaten to death and that got them mad enough to take on the Young Guns."

He agreed with Greg Ridd that their security men should continue to work in pairs, until they were sure that there was no likelihood of more attacks. The helmets and sprays would now be permanent equipment to make their men the best protected in the city. With the threat to his security operation removed and the problems at the Hungarian mine settled, Jack thought he could relax and continue building his Liverpool business and enjoying life with his growing family. He could not know that one man's stupidity and another man's frustration would soon result in further deaths and destruction.

Chapter 18
Consummation

After Theresa and her mother Mary were rescued from the squalor of the run-down trailer park in Canada by her uncle, Jack Randil, she began a new life with the family in Liverpool and took every advantage of the opportunities available to her. She had always dreamed that one day she would fall in love and lead a happy, normal life, even when she was surrounded by rusting trailers and discarded rubbish heaps. When Demeter flew to Liverpool and she met him for the first time, it was love at first sight. He was tall, dark and handsome, as well as sensitive and charming and she knew he was the one she wanted to marry. She pursued him, but knew that he was attracted to her and when they finally became engaged, she felt that her dreams had come true.

Since she had only her carry-on luggage, she was one of the first passengers from the flight to head for the exit and easily recognised the tall figure of her fiancée standing near the barrier. She ran up to him, threw her arms around him and kissed him full on the lips. The elegantly dressed man tried to hide his embarrassment, but nevertheless held her tightly and responded to her kiss. The twelve-year age gap and difference in their cultures made him less open with his feelings than Theresa, but his eyes and embrace showed his strong feelings for the vivacious young woman. Her only luggage was a small carry-on bag and he took it from her as they walked to the car park.

On the way to the hotel, Theresa wanted to know all about progress at the mine and if the problems which had worried her fiancée had now been resolved. Demeter gave her uncle, Jack Randil, full credit for persuading Radics to finally compromise in his handling of the Roma community. Theresa laughed when she heard this and told him that Jack could be very persuasive and always seemed able to find a simple solution to a problem.

Her mother had told her about the gang war in Liverpool and that some of Jack's security team had been attacked. Demeter was surprised to hear about the on-going violence in Liverpool, since Jack had told him nothing during his recent visit for the Hun-Al board meeting.

"If he knew that you had problems, he wouldn't want to burden you with hearing about his as well, but he always seems to come out on top. I know of lots of people who have tried to cause trouble for him and found themselves far worse off. Now tell me what you have planned for us in this beautiful city, which you claim is the most attractive in Europe."

"First you must see the hotel, which I have chosen specially to impress you because it is also elegant and beautiful, just like you."

She squeezed his hand and laughed and then she caught her first sight of the Corinthia Hotel, which was a five-story stone building with an elegant entrance which dominated the surrounding buildings in the city centre. After Demeter had parked his car, they walked into the beautifully tiled reception area, which Theresa immediately thought had Moorish antecedents. The attractive receptionist carried on a long and very friendly conversation with Demeter, and Theresa decided that either they knew each other well, or the receptionist was hoping she would. Since she spoke no Hungarian, she had no idea as to what was being said. Demeter had booked adjoining rooms and she found that she could look out on the city from her window. She saw that there was a door between her own and Demeter's room.

Since it was late afternoon, as soon as Theresa was settled in, Demeter suggested that they take a walk across the chain bridge, which linked Buda with Pest. The sun was shining, but there was already a bite in the air as autumn had ended and they were both well wrapped up against the chill. From the bridge they had a clear view of the Danube and the striking outline of the buildings along the shoreline on each bank. The walk and the fresh air gave them appetites and Demeter explained that the Hungarian hotel had a superb restaurant to give Theresa her first taste of the delicious local cuisine.

Knowing that they would have at least one formal occasion, she had packed a figure-hugging black dress bought by her mother as a combined Xmas, birthday and engagement present. It was the most expensive dress she had ever owned, but after her mother urged her to try it on in spite of the high price, she could not refuse. There was an iron in a cupboard of her room and she used it to smooth out the creases after taking it from her small bag. When Demeter tapped on her door to take her down to the restaurant, he could not prevent his eyes from straying to her superb figure, which was emphasised by the dress. With her lustrous black, shoulder length hair and green eyes, he knew that she would attract most of the men in the restaurant.

He had reserved a corner table and since he always stayed at the hotel during his regular visits to the city, the maître d'hôtel knew him and greeted the couple before personally showing them to their table. Demeter explained in English that it was Theresa's first visit and experience of Hungarian cuisine. The man bowed and welcomed her to the hotel and assured her that they would do their very best to provide her with superb food. The menu was extensive and written in Hungarian, so Demeter called out the selections with the English translation and laughed at the bewildered expression on his fiancé's face as she told him.

"You order darling and I will have whatever you choose. I am so hungry and it all sounds so delicious that I know I will like it."

"Very well, let's begin with *halászlé*, fisherman's soup with red fish, spiced with paprika. To follow I think *stefánia szelet*, a meatloaf with hard boiled eggs in the middle and to finish, *gundel palacsinta*, which is a crepe stuffed with walnuts, flambéed in a chocolate sauce."

"Sounds wonderful, if I can get through it all."

"Once you taste, you will not be able to stop I am sure. Now, what wine would you like?"

They settled on a white dessert wine, Tokaji and their waiter lit the glass-framed candle in the centre of their table, just as a string quartet began to play in the restaurant. As Theresa looked across the table into the dark eyes of her man, she knew that her long-time dream had come true. The food and the atmosphere made her feel that she had been transported to wonderland. After the meal they decided to take coffee in the lounge and relax, since they were both feeling drowsy after their busy day and the wine they drank during dinner.

After drinking their coffee, they sat and talked in the elegant lounge and then walked arm in arm to their rooms. At her bedroom door, Demeter took her in his arms and their bodies pressed hard against each other in a goodnight embrace. Theresa could feel Demeter's enlarged passion and was yearning to open her door and make love, but knew that it was too soon. She pulled away and pressed her fingers against Demeter's lips and said goodnight before going into her bedroom alone.

After breakfast, they took a taxi and walked around Margaret Island, which had once been a royal hunting ground and was covered with 10,000 trees amongst beautiful gardens and a unique musical fountain. Afterwards they visited St Stephens Basilica and the Zoo, which opened in 1866 and watched the enclosed area designed to allow children to watch the cubs of many of the zoo animals. Demeter had booked seats for the evening performance of the Budapest Municipal Circus in City Park, the first public park in the world. The circus was housed in a large stone building with space for an audience of up to 1850 persons. After another exquisite meal in the hotel restaurant they went to their rooms and agreed to make an early start for the drive to the Pusztai mansion at Dunakeszi.

When Demeter moved in to the family home, he had employed a middle-aged couple to live in and look after his needs. Aranka was his housekeeper and cook and her husband, Janos, was a handyman who helped Demeter in his restoration work on the building. He had saved money when he was employed as a senior engineer working for Renault in France and he now had a reasonable salary from his position in Hun-Al so that he could afford to employ tradesmen to do the more complicated repairs, beginning with the roof. The building was now sound and many of the rooms were furnished, but the decorating would take many months to complete. Anticipating Theresa's visit, he had raced to make his home presentable, if not anywhere near its original elegance.

When Theresa saw the house for the first time, she immediately felt that it matched her dreams. It was a two-story stone building with a red-tiled roof and an extended entrance porch set in the middle, to shelter visitors using the front door. Theresa imagined carriages stopping under the porch and guests stepping down to walk inside the house. Demeter parked his car on the gravelled drive and as they entered the house, they were met by Aranka. The large woman gave Theresa a big hug and welcomed her speaking in Hungarian, which Demeter translated. After settling in to her room, she and Demeter walked around the house and looked at the ruins of the stable block, which had been burned down to draw Demeter to the house so that Roma assassins could kill him, but fortunately Jack had been on hand to stop them. Janos had gone into town for supplies.

As they looked at the blackened ruins, Demeter described how the building had once been used to stable up to twelve horses, most of them plough horses used on the land, but some for his grandmother and grandfather to ride. He told her how, after giving birth to his father Istvan and while out riding her favourite horse, his grandmother had been thrown and killed after a Roma woman flared her red skirts to deliberately frighten the horse. She too had the same lustrous black hair as Theresa and had been just as athletic and determined.

"How terrible for your father. When I was at school, I was given riding lessons and afterwards, worked at the local stable and mucked out the stalls to be allowed free rides."

"Wonderful. I have ridden since I was a small boy and will borrow some horses so that we can explore the Pusztai lands together tomorrow. A lot of the horse tack and saddles were saved from the fire and perhaps, I can also find you some riding boots. One day, we may build new stables and have our own horses to ride the land together."

That evening they ate in the large dining room and enjoyed the meal prepared by Aranka, which was served by husband Janos. He was nervous when first introduced to Theresa and bowed and forgot to release her hand, then hovered near her and attended to her every request, translated by Demeter. The house had a veranda at the rear and they sat on a wooden bench and drank the sweet local coffee as they looked across the fields and low hills surrounding the house.

"I think you have captivated Janos too, so now you have two men willing to meet your every wish my darling."

"Janos is a lovely man, but too old for me, I shall have to work my wicked ways with you instead, so watch out."

Demeter held her hand as they walked up the wide stairway and turned to leave as they reached her bedroom door. She reached out to take his hand and then drew him inside her room. This would be their home and this was the time to make him her lover. At breakfast next morning, Theresa saw Aranka's knowing smile and knew that she had guessed that one bedroom would be all that was needed in future.

After breakfast, the horses were saddled and the two lovers rode off together under a blue sky, but with a cool wind sweeping across the land. Demeter was a natural rider and she knew she would have difficulty keeping up with him. She suggested a short ride to avoid saddle burn. They were cantering down a shallow slope with Demeter slightly in front when suddenly there was the sound of a shot. Theresa's horse jerked its head up and stumbled before collapsing and throwing her from the saddle.

Demeter immediately jumped from his horse and raced back to find Theresa lying flat on her back in the long grass. As he cradled her shoulders in his arms, he was relieved to see her open her eyed and smile at him.

"Don't worry darling, I'm alright, but I think I have done something to my arm, would you please see how the horse is. I think he was shot."

Glancing at the horse lying motionless nearby, he could see the blood covering its eye and open mouth and knew it had been shot through the head. There was no movement in its chest and he was sure it was dead. Checking her arm, he thought it was probably broken and he took off his jacket and used it to strap her arm against her breast, since he could see that any movement caused her pain. Her face was also bruised and scratched, but he was relieved that she had survived without critical injuries. Telling her to lie down in a small fold in the ground, he looked for the shooter and saw a horseman riding hard to leave the scene. He helped her up onto his horse and they began the two-mile walk back to the house. He was furious with himself for risking her life by thinking that the problems with the local Roma had been settled.

It was late afternoon by the time they reached the mansion, and Aranka and Janos were shocked that anyone would try to shoot the young woman. They decided that rather than call out the local doctor, he would drive Theresa to the small hospital in the town to have her injuries attended to. The staff were very helpful, but the police were called and Demeter had to explain the shooting. He was more worried about Theresa than trying to locate, or identify the shooter who had left after firing one shot. With hindsight, he began to appreciate that they could both have been killed if the gunman had carried on firing. In future he would always carry a gun wherever he went.

After her arm was splinted up and bandaged at the hospital, they returned to the mansion and Demeter insisted that first thing next morning, he would drive her to the airport for the flight home. They had scarcely made this decision when Demeter received a frantic telephone call from Larjos to tell him that Radics had arrested Boldo and it had resulted in an all-out battle with the Roma. Hearing this, Demeter booked Theresa on a first-class flight to Manchester, where he knew her family would be able to meet her. He charged the amount to the Hun-Al account, since it was Radic's actions which had led to the problems with local Roma and her wounding. The extra space and comfort would certainly make her flight more bearable after her brief visit. He could not understand how the commissar had again allowed his prejudice to put the entire mining project in jeopardy by arresting the Roma leader. Demeter knew Boldo well and had always found him a mild mannered, harmless and friendly man.

During the evening, Theresa's eye began to turn black as the bruise to her forehead spread and she teased Demeter by telling him she could always accuse him of beating her. Seeing the horror on his face, she immediately reassured him that she was only joking. He telephoned Jack Randil and told him about the shooting and the cause. His friend asked for full details and when told that they were riding downhill, he guessed the shooter was not experienced and had not adequately allowed for their forward movement, or descent. Since Theresa's following horse was shot in the head, he believed that Demeter had been the target and it had been a bad miss. Thankfully, his niece was not seriously injured, but now instead of damaging property, the Roma were targeting people. He had some clearing up to do in Liverpool after recent problems, but would fly to Budapest in two days' time.

Demeter was very subdued during their evening together because he felt it was his fault for putting Theresa in danger. As a consequence, he would now only have four days of her company. She did her best to convince him that both he and her

Uncle Jack had thought the problems at the mine were over. He should not blame himself when it was entirely the fault of the man Radics for again stirring up trouble with the local Roma just when the mine was back in production. They shared one bedroom for their last night together and both took great care to protect her broken arm.

Chapter 19
Confrontation

The two Romanian policemen had begun moving north after starting their search in the small villages south of Bacău. Bumbesco reasoned that the Tigani people, who had been driven from Budestin when it was burned, would probably settle in existing Tigani settlements in the general area of Bacău, or in small groups in the open country.

If Tigo had returned from his travels to find his people scattered and his mother killed, he would probably return to them after murdering those he blamed as responsible. As their leader, he would want to gather as many as possible into a new community to re-establish his control over them.

Rudi was moving slowly north amongst the Tigani settlements and using his mechanical talents to repair appliances, or even their cars, to pick up local gossip but avoid appearing too inquisitive. Although horses were still an important part of Tigani life, the motor car was seen as a status symbol, even if the engine did not work. Rudi was fixing the magneto on a battered Lada when his sharp ears picked up a conversation, which mentioned the name Tigo. Moving around the car and keeping his head under the bonnet, he managed to get closer to hear more. One Tigani was complaining to another that he had been regularly beaten by Tigo. He had moved his family away from Budestin, only to find his persecutor travelling around the area to bully his people again and rebuild the community at Pasiti, which Rudi sensed was not far away.

After switching on the engine and seeing the Tigani owner swell with pride that he could again sit inside and rev up the engine, even if he was not intending to drive anywhere. Rudi accepted payment in food for the night and to take with him when he left the following morning. Sitting around the campfire as he ate his stew and bread with the others, Rudi asked where he might find more work in nearby settlements, or villages. Three, or four names were mentioned, including Pasiti. Wanting to avoid showing any interest in the town where Tigo was now living, he asked for details about a number and included Pasiti as he compared the size and distances involved. Having obtained all the information he needed, he decided to travel to a town where he could meet Bumbesco and pass on what he had learned. The lieutenant would then decide on the next course of action.

Early the following morning, Rudi drove his horse and vardo along the road leading to Moineşti, which was the nearest town where he expected to be able to telephone Bumbesco to arrange a meeting. He was moving in the rough direction of Pasiti, but knew it would be unwise for him to travel there alone before discussing the best course of action with his boss. They were stalking a murderer who had shown he would kill without hesitation. Rudi had hidden a revolver inside the vardo, but this would be no match for a rifle, which had been used to shoot the commissar. If he had to engage Tigo in physical combat, he had no doubt that he would be able to subdue, or even kill the man.

The weather was surprisingly good and he hoped to reach Moineşti by the next morning by getting off to an early start. It had been just ten days since he had first begun his search for the elusive Tigo and now they could be close to finding him. Just as he was beginning to think they would not find their quarry; the chance remark had pointed the way. He wondered if he would qualify for the reward if they arrested Tigo. As late afternoon approached, he could tell that the horse needed a rest and decided to pull over to the side of the road and stop overnight. He chose an open space at the edge of the forest. There was good grazing for his horse and a stream nearby to provide it with water. He unhitched the horse and tied a rope to the halter to connect it to the vardo and prevent it wandering off, but within reach of the stream.

He collected dried wood from the forest and was setting a fire to make tea when he heard the familiar noise of wild boars in the distance. The noise was coming closer and he knew how dangerous the vicious animals could be. He thought about getting his revolver, but the animals moved so quickly and he was such a poor marksman that he knew it would be pointless.

Instead he took hold of a spade, which he used to level sites for the vardo and waited near the horse. He could not untie the halter because the animal had already sensed the wild boar approach and would gallop off if untied. Suddenly, a large wild boar with prominent tusks broke through the bushes and he watched as it paused and its red eyes looked around the clearing. The frightened horse reared up on its hind legs and snorted. The sudden movement and noise attracted the boar and it charged.

Rudi stood between the horse and the boar with the spade cocked at shoulder level. Timing his strike, he swung the spade and connected with the head of the boar so that it was knocked sideways and rolled over screaming wildly. It landed near the stream and went silent and Rudi was sure he had killed it. It was a magnificent strike, but unfortunately the noise alerted the rest of the boars, which began streaming out of the forest. Rudi feared for his own and the horse's life against a combined attack by the creatures. He raised the spade again and prepared to kill, or maim as many as possible. Suddenly, there was a shot and a boar dropped flat, then another boar was shot and killed and the pack turned and raced for safety in the forest. Looking for his rescuer, Rudi watched as a tall man holding a rifle stepped down from his horse and walked towards him with the rifle held across his chest. The stranger was bearded and his shoulder length black hair was oiled and braided.

"Light your fire traveller, and we will have boar for supper."

The man walked past to reach down and grab hold of a tusk and drag a boar towards Rudi who noticed the distinctive Tigani clothes and thanked him by speaking in the Romani language.

"Thank you for frightening them off. They normally keep clear of people. I didn't expect the old boar to charge, but I think the horse startled him and I don't know whether the rest were charging, or running away, but now we have plenty to eat."

"I saw your grand vardo and watched you kill the big boar leader and wanted to talk to you, but the rest ran out of the forest and gave us our supper. Where are you going?"

"I hope to reach Moinești in the morning and find some repair work, since I was told it was a good place for Tigani."

"I want to take two boars to my people who are at Pasiti, which is near Moinești. One boar is yours, but the other two are mine and their meat is very good. You build up the fire and I will cut up your boar for supper."

The horseman unsaddled the stallion and hitched it to one of the wheels of the vardo, then moved all three boar carcasses to lie near the front wheels. Taking out a large knife he began slicing meat from the big boar for their evening meal. Rudi got a fire going and sharpened some sticks to use in barbecuing the pork. Pulling a battered black metal pot from a cupboard, he filled it with water from the stream and hung it over the fire to boil and make tea. Next, he brought two small wooden stools out of the vardo and set them near the fire. The pork smelled delicious and once the tea was made the two men ate the food by using their knives and washed the food down with the strong black tea.

"There are not many vardos like the one you have. I have never seen another like it. Our people are beginning to build houses and use cheap caravans and some have cars to pull them. How long have you been travelling in this area?"

Rudi and Bumbesco had discussed a cover story in case anyone was suspicious of a traveller suddenly appearing in the area and Rudi sensed that it was just as well he was prepared.

"I work in Focsani as a car mechanic and the vardo belonged to my grandfather. When he died, he left it to my father, but he had made my father promise to drive the vardo for a month to help to keep the old traditions going. We have worked to restore the vardo for the past year and my father and I were going to make the journey together, but he is ill and insisted that I go on my own. My journey is almost finished and after I make some money in Moineşti, I will be going back to Focsani."

"Come to Pasiti with me and bring the boars and I will make sure you have plenty of work to earn money. When you have finished the work, you can go home. My name is Tigo and I am the leader of a group of Tigani in Pasiti."

Rudi had already suspected that he might have met their quarry by chance. The man was big and obviously accustomed to having his own way and very few Tigani had guns and certainly not hunting rifles. If he refused the invitation, the man could well shoot him and take over the vardo. Better to accept and try to find some way of contacting Bumbesco, who had not heard from him for over a week.

"That is a good offer and there are two bunks in the vardo if you would like to spend the night here. I will follow you to Pasiti in the morning."

After finishing supper, Tigo said that the smell of the cooking food could be picked up by a bear half a mile away. Once it got the scent, it would certainly come to seek food. The horses could be at risk and to protect them he would lie near the fire and keep watch. He would wake if any beasts came sniffing around and would drive them off, or shoot them. Just after midnight, Rudi was shaken awake and told to take his turn guarding the horses. Tigo kept the gun with him and told Rudi that from the top of the vardo steps, he would have a clear shot at any troublesome beasts. Although this sounded reasonable, Rudi did not like having a killer with a rifle above him while he tried to sleep.

After his night watch, Rudi was stiff and tired because he had not been able to sleep during the five hours and as the fire had gone out, he was also cold. Tigo awoke early and told him to make the fire while he watered the horses and led them to an area of good grass for them to graze. The two men drank tea together and cooked some more strips of pork before preparing the horses for the journey to Pasiti. The boar carcasses had stopped seeping blood and after washing them in the stream he wrapped them in an old blanket and placed them on the floor of the vardo. Tigo told him that they would be prepared and cooked by his people for eating. They arrived at Pasiti three hours later and although the stranger in the vardo was welcomed, especially when they saw the boars, the return of their leader Tigo did not appear to be appreciated by all those meeting them. Rudi hoped that this would help him if he could contact Bumbesco and they arrested Tigo.

Releasing his horse from its harness and setting up the vardo for his stay, he was offered at least three days' work and soon got to know the locals, who all wanted to look at the vardo and talk to him about other villages he had visited. He was aware of Tigo watching him from time to time as he was cleaning his rifle, then saw the leader walk off into the forest. He tried to do work for those who appeared to dislike Tigo, whether by a look, or a chance remark. He was trying to rebuild the carburettor on an old Dacia car for Pesha, who was a small chatty man who stood beside the car as Rudi worked on the engine. Pesha told him that they had been driven from the village where they lived by soldiers and Rudi smiled, but said nothing. Rudi continued his work and the man then said that he did not like being in Pasiti and if Rudi could fix his car, he might leave.

"How long did you live in your other village Pesha?"

"I was born there and grew up with Tigo, but he was a bully and his older step brother was just as bad, but he is dead now."

Rudi looked carefully around the site for any sign of Tigo, but he seemed to be still in the forest. Although anxious to learn more he knew that he must avoid asking direct questions, but keep Pesha talking about the old village.

"After the Russians left our country, I thought we would be safe, but now you tell me that our own soldiers attacked your village for no reason."

"There was bad blood between the brothers, but Tigo was leader although he was younger. The older brother Renko killed the son of a chief in France and he sent men to punish Renko. Tigo held a trial and his brother was found guilty and he was nailed to a wooden board. The French Tigani must have talked about it and the soldiers came to find what happened. They were also looking for another Tigani, who never spoke very much, who had come to our village a few weeks before."

Tigo suddenly appeared from the back of the car with a face red with anger. As he strode towards Pesha, the small man cowered in fright and Tigo smashed his fist into the face of the small man, who fell to the ground unconscious. His nose and mouth a mass of blood.

"This fool is a gossip and you don't want to take notice of his lies. Come, there are other things to fix and you should not waste your time working on this heap of metal."

After kicking the Dacia car, Tigo took hold of Rudi by the arm and pulled him over to the other side of the village, not looking at the inert body of Pesha on the ground. Rudi made up his mind to say nothing about Pesha's comments and be very careful not to ask any questions. He thought that if Tigo now wanted to prevent the details of his brother's death reaching the authorities, he would have no hesitation in killing Rudi, but not while he was in Pasiti, where there were too many witnesses. The most likely danger time would come when he left the village and was driving through the forest. Fortunately, he had his revolver, but this would not be very effective against a rifle in the hands of a hidden marksman.

He picked up a reward notice, which had obviously been torn down from a tree trunk and thrown amongst some rubbish. He slipped it into his pocket and would try to find which of the Tigani's could read and then somehow leave the notice where he was likely to find it and hopefully read it. He knew his life was in danger and he had to find every possible way of helping himself to survive. He carved two wooden wedges to jam his door at night, in case Tigo came to slit his throat. He also kept his revolver where he could get hold of it quickly.

Bumbesco had been making his way north on a parallel course to Rudi, but driving along the edge of the mountains so that he could drive, or walk along the valleys to hunt. He was choosing pheasants to shoot because they were good targets and small enough for him to cook for his lunch in the forest. At night he ate in the hotel, or the inn where he slept. He saw deer and an ibis, but they were large animals and the government wanted them protected. He was waiting to hear from Rudi and although he understood that it was sometimes difficult, it was now ten days since the big policeman had set off in his vardo. He tried not to think about the disappearance of the last Tigani sent to check on Tigo's actions.

He could not begin visiting local Tigani communities without putting his man in danger, but his daily routine was beginning to bore him and the lack of constructive action was making him frustrated. He had received two telephone calls from Major Chisca to ask about their progress and in the last call the previous day, his boss was obviously not impressed to hear that he had no idea where Rudi was. A fox ran across the trail in front of him and he immediately shot it and then felt guilty for killing the poor animal because of his frustration. He must maintain his control and let the investigation proceed according to his original plan. Having tired of pheasant, he kept watch for an alternative and when a group of wild boars ran past, he shot one of the smaller, younger boars. There were quite a few in the forest and he liked their meat. He would put the carcass in his car and take it back to have his landlord prepare it and share it with others at the inn.

It was late afternoon and he lifted the boar into the back of the Suzuki and wrapped it in a groundsheet before beginning his drive back. He was staying the night at a small inn on a minor road passing through the town of Comăneşti, which was adjacent to the area where Rudi should be travelling. So far, the reward offer for information about Tigo had brought no results. The leaflets had been widely distributed, but many Tigani were unable to read. It was also possible that those who knew, or were living near Tigo were too frightened to contact the authorities and possibly risk their lives.

After a delicious evening meal of pig cooked on a revolving spit and helped down with local beer, Bumbesco returned to his room feeling guilty at his comfortable part in the search. He could not continue waiting when Rudi could be in danger. After studying a local map and calculating the average rate of progress he tried to find a town where Rudi might go to contact him, even if he had yet to gather any information on Tigo.

Chapter 20
Attrition

The Russian Mafia gang had all been killed and Jack Randil was able to reassure customers protected by his security operation that there would be no further night-time burglaries, or fires at their properties. Greg Ridd was relieved that the threat to his team had been removed, but was also pleased that their systems had been tested and as a result, their training methods and equipment had been improved. Staff who had been attacked received bonuses and were now fully recovered and back at work.

Theresa was recuperating at home after being collected at the airport by her stepfather Greg Ridd and her Uncle Jack Randil. Judy was worried that her husband was once again putting himself at risk by flying back to Hungary to try to stop the war between the local Roma people and the Hun-Al mining staff. Greg and Mary were furious that their daughter had escaped being shot by just three feet. Jack with Theresa's help had to work hard to convince them that their future son in law was now in danger and needed their support. Greg then insisted that he should join Jack on his peacekeeping mission, but seeing the concern in his sister's eyes, Jack wanted to avoid taking his friend into danger.

"There will have to be a board meeting to pressure Radics to stop mixing his politics with Hun-Al operations and we should then be able to reach agreement with the Roma. We should not be fighting with the Roma when like us they just want to live their lives in peace. You are needed here to help to settle our security business after the run in with the Russians."

Jack Randil flew alone to Budapest and was met at the airport by Demeter, who immediately apologised for believing that his home in Dunakeszi was safe for Theresa and risking her life. Jack assured him that he could not have known that Radics had literally destroyed the agreement by arresting Boldo and provoking the Roma people to retaliate. Demeter explained the details as they drove north to the mine offices.

"After the rail track was routed away from the village the people slowly returned and Boldo was once again their leader and living amongst them. Ore production was increasing and with the track almost reaching the mine, the company would soon have been able to move greater quantities of ore to the refining plant at lower cost.

"Commissar Radics in his official capacity claimed that government property had been destroyed and that those responsible were certainly Roma. Since the damage had been done at night by saboteurs, it was not possible to punish individuals, but as the leader, Boldo must be held responsible. Police arrested him and he was locked up in the Dunakeszi police cells.

"The night of his arrest marked the start of a new wave of destruction. Explosions at both the mine and the refinery totally stopped ore production and more than twenty security men were overpowered and tied up as the explosive charges were placed. Radics refused to accept responsibility for the stoppage, or to discuss the release of Boldo. The rail track was not touched, but work to extend it to the mine was stopped on Radics orders."

Jack listened to the account of the problems and then began to look for gaps and possible moves, which would repair the goodwill of the Roma people.

"So yet again there have been no casualties in spite of the damage and the provocation. Has anyone been inside the jail to speak with Boldo and has a board meeting been called to discuss the crisis?"

"You are right Jack; the Roma obviously want to avoid harming anyone and so far in spite of the explosions there are no casualties. It seems to be a dispute about property and so far, no one has been to speak with Boldo. I have been trying to check the damage since Theresa went back to Manchester and have not had time to speak to Boldo, but there will be a board meeting in two days' time when all the members reach the mine offices."

"Good, that gives us time to meet Boldo before the meeting. Since care was taken to avoid casualties, why then did someone try to kill you and nearly hit Theresa. Is there something else going on that we don't know about? There have been attempts on your life for years, but after Renko was killed we were sure you were safe at last, but perhaps we were wrong."

"Renko was born to a Roma woman who worked hard to send him to school and as you know, he became the Police Chief here in Dunakeszi. His mother Bella is dead now, but there are still some relatives living in the area in the house which she owned. Bella had a daughter and a son besides Renko, but I have never thought they were a threat to my family. When we speak with Boldo, I will sound him out about any locals who might want to harm me."

When they reached the Pusztai mansion, Jack met Aranka for the first time and as Demeter took him around the house to show off the renovation work, he also met Janos. Thanks to his limited knowledge of Hungarian, Jack was able to respond when the couple asked how Theresa was after falling from her horse. Demeter had hired them the day Jack left after the last board meeting and Janos was a hard worker who had finished replacing the windows and doors, whilst a contractor had completed repairs on the roof.

Work was proceeding to repair the damage inflicted by the Roma on mine property and they decided to visit Boldo to find a way to end the attacks.

The Police Chief also wanted to see an end to the trouble and when they asked to see Boldo, he had the elderly Roma brought from his cell and allowed them to use his office for the meeting. Coffee was provided and they were sure that the prisoner was being treated very kindly, in spite of Commissar Radic's instructions. Boldo shook hands with them both and told them he was sure that they had nothing to do with his imprisonment. He knew they would come to see him and he had something for them to use in stopping Radics from ruining the mine and his village. He explained.

"Bella was a beautiful Romanian woman who arrived here already pregnant with Renko and as a Roma, she was made welcome to live amongst us. She was a hard worker and earned enough to send her son to school. You know she worked as a maid for your grandparents and she caused your grandmother's death by frightening her horse. She tricked your grandfather into

112

marrying her by pretending she was a single young Romanian woman and then invited her Roma sister and her son Renko into the Pusztai house. Your grandfather was furious and threw her out and had the marriage annulled. Bella, Renko and her sister moved back to our village and when he was eighteen Renko began working for the Communists. He was ruthless and brutal and soon earned promotions and a transfer to the secret police.

"Over the years when communism was strong, he forced people to tell him their secrets and become his informers. He became a senior officer, but when communism was swept away, many members of the secret police were killed by people taking revenge. Renko was never punished for his crimes, but instead was appointed as Dunakeszi Police Chief, because he knew the past secrets of those who took over the new government. He was forced out of this position for trying to kill you and your sister by hiring two assassins. He was warned by someone in the government that he was to be arrested. This allowed him to escape and hide many of his files in the family house where Bella's sister lives."

Boldo passed Demeter a bulky envelope with the name Radics written on the front and told him to read it and use the information to force the commissar to resign from the mining company. There were quite a few papers inside and Demeter asked if Boldo knew what they showed.

"Commissar Radics claims he worked for the West German police force when Hungary was controlled by the Russian communists, but it was the East German police and he was a Stasi officer serving in East Berlin and guilty of many crimes. He could not find these papers when Renko escaped to Romania, but guessed they were hidden somewhere in our village and wanted it destroyed by using the rail track."

Pointing at Jack he told him that he had forced Radics to move the track around the village to avoid looking as if he wanted the Roma to continue disrupting mining.

"When I returned to the Roma village, he arrested me to break the agreement and provoke my people, but by then I had found Renko's store of secrets."

The two men were shocked to hear the truth about Radics, but the man was an important government official and they would have to find a way of removing him, but prevent him learning of their intentions and using his power against them. Jack had an idea, but wanted to work through the papers Boldo had given them before sharing it with Demeter, to avoid raising false hopes. Turning to Boldo, he told him about the shooting of Theresa's horse and his belief that Demeter had been the actual target. He asked him whether he knew of any Roma who wanted to kill Demeter. Boldo was silent while he thought over the question and then gave them his answer.

"Bella Veres was pregnant when she arrived here from Romania and gave birth to the boy Renko Veres. After being driven out of the big house and divorced, she lived with a local Roma who fathered a son and a daughter from her, but she never married her man. The man Pista lives in the village and has a family, but has never been in any trouble. He does not own a gun and I think he would not know how to use it even if he had one. Renko believed that he was cheated out of inheriting the Pusztai lands by your father Istvan and tried to kill you and your sister so that he would be the only one with a claim. Pista has never said he wanted to claim the land and does not have your blood link Demeter. Renko had a younger brother, who lived with his father who was a Roma chief in Romania. I don't think he ever visited Dunakeszi and he does not have a blood claim either. He succeeded Renko's father as the chief, although Renko was the oldest son. There was bad blood between the two brothers and Renko was killed."

"What about the silent Romanian who was with you at our last meeting?"

"Gunari is a Roma who wants to help his people to stand up for themselves and stop being treated as second class citizens. He is a highly trained soldier who has seen far less qualified soldiers promoted, but remained a private because he is a Roma. He has learned Hungarian and has spoken with dozens of Roma communities in the area and is accepted by them as a leader. He knows you try to look after us and would have no reason to attack you. He is a fine shot and he would not have missed if he wanted to shoot you. He first came here with a tall man some months ago and then returned to help us when I heard rumours about the rail running through our village. I asked for his help and he came."

After thanking Boldo for giving them the evidence on Radics and answering their questions, they assured him that they hoped to free him soon and restore the good relations with him and his people. They also thanked the Police Chief for being helpful, but said nothing about the papers given to them by Boldo. When they returned to the mine office, they locked the door and began working through the papers. Renko had been very thorough and there were official documents and witness statements, which fully incriminated Commissar Radics. Jack then outlined his idea for removing Radics.

"Dorika Biro was appointed to the board by the government and she supported us when we were trying to get Radics to reroute the rail line around the Roma village. She is a professional and knows the country needs the foreign exchange from the mine. Can we talk to her before the board meeting and show her the evidence? With her support we can force Radics to resign and get things working again. If the government wants to avoid bad publicity, Radics can claim to be giving up his seat on the board and his position as Police Commissioner due to ill health."

Demeter telephoned Dorika at her office in Budapest and they arranged to drive to the city and talk with her later in the afternoon.

They had to wait for a meeting to finish before being shown in to her office and she was obviously not happy about seeing them to discuss board matters before the meeting the next day. Demeter showed her the documents, which listed the most serious charges. He then explained how Radics was deliberately inciting the Romas to try to hide the evidence on his past and putting the mine output at risk. Her eyes blazed with anger and she made it clear that she would certainly not allow Radics to quietly retire and instead wanted him to pay for his crimes and go to prison. She thanked them for bringing her the papers and for their real concern over maintaining mine output. She also assured them that Radics would immediately be arrested.

The board meeting was held the following day, but Radics was not present. Dorika proposed a vote of confidence in Demeter for identifying the cause of mine disruptions and providing evidence, which would result in the imprisonment of the culprit. Boldo was released the same day and it was hoped that the mine would be back in full production within two weeks and making full use of the direct rail link between the mine and refinery. Demeter was delighted that his problems were over and he had restored relations with the local Roma. Jack still had concerns.

"The mine should now have no more problems, but you and I need to meet this non speaking Romanian, Gunari and fill in some gaps, unless you want to continue being a target for a hidden rifleman. We have to find out why and who, before we can make you safe and Theresa can live at Dunakeszi."

They drove to the Roma settlement and the people smiled and waved to them as they walked towards the house where Boldo lived. Obviously, the word had quickly spread about their success in having Radics arrested and saving the village from destruction. Boldo hugged both men and agreed to invite Gunari to come and meet them at his house. The Romanian was away and he did not say where, or what he was doing, but he again reassured Demeter that he was sure that Gunari meant him no harm. He invited them to return the next day at the same time and Gunari should be there to speak with them. They left the village and for the rest of the day they toured the mine, refinery and rail track to check on the progress of the repair work.

Chapter 21
Confrontation

Rudi repaired the diesel engine on an old Mercedes army lorry, which must have been abandoned when the Germans retreated from the Russian army, sweeping south from Ukraine. Dirty fuel had totally clogged the system and the engine had to be almost rebuilt. Rudi was pleased with his work and the Tigani owner thought he was a magician to bring the old engine back to life. Pesha walked over when he heard the distinctive noise of the diesel engine coming to life and he smiled in spite of his two black eyes and swollen nose.

"You have special skill in those hands Rudi and thanks to you I am driving in my motor car to the fair at Moineşti this morning."

Rudi wanted to avoid making too much contact with Pesha to save him from further beatings from Tigo, but the small man was obviously proud to own a car and was naturally friendly.

"Do not drive too fast and smash it up after all my hard work and have a good time at the fair."

Watching Pesha laughing as he walked back to his car and began loading it, Rudi switched off the army lorry engine to make some adjustments and asked the owner what he would be doing at the fair. He was startled to hear that Pesha had been to school and was a clever wood carver who made wooden dolls, which his wife dressed and then they were sold at fairs in the area. They were in demand and the couple made a good living. Rudi immediately saw an opportunity and walked over to Pesha alongside the car.

"Let me make sure that you will be able to reach the fair and get back."

Working under the bonnet he opened the reward notice so that Pesha, who was standing alongside, was able to read it. Rudi watched as he saw the surprised expression on his face, followed by a gleam in his eyes as he realised that Rudi was giving him the means to take revenge on Tigo. Satisfied that he had set things in motion, he folded the notice and slipped it alongside the battery where it could be retrieved, but not seen. He closed the bonnet.

"This car could take you to Budapest if you knew the way and had enough petrol. I hope you do well in Moineşti Pesha."

The Roma nodded his head to Rudi and then he and his wife climbed into the car and Rudi watched as it drove off and bounced over the rough track taking them away from Pasiti. The noise of the high revving engine must have awakened Tigo, who appeared at his door, shirtless, with tousled hair and bloodshot eyes after a bout of hard drinking the previous night. Looking around the area, he slowly appreciated that Pesha's car was no longer outside his house and asked where he had gone. When he learned that Pesha had driven to Moineşti, Rudi could see the frown appear on Tigo's face as he worked out possible implications. Seeing Rudi working on the Mercedes lorry he asked if it would now work and the proud owner told him that it had just been running and made a great sound.

Tigo went back into his house and returned a few minutes later fully dressed and holding the hunting rifle across his chest. Waving the gun at the owner, he told him to start the Mercedes and take him to Moineşti now. Knowing that it was unwise to argue, the man told Rudi to close the bonnet and he and Tigo sat in the cab and the engine then fired and the lorry moved slowly forward. Rudi had already seen that the tyres were almost flat and should have been pumped up, but had been given no opportunity to warn the lorry owner. He was sure that the lorry would be far slower than the car and could well suffer a flat tyre. He hoped Pesha would go straight to the Moineşti police station with the information, which could bring him the large reward. Realising that he had been given the ideal opportunity to leave without risking a confrontation with Tigo, he harnessed his horse, put his tools in the vardo and after waving goodbye to the villagers, he headed down the track. As he drove along the rutted surface, he kept a close watch in front to be ready if the lorry was stranded. Tigo had taken his gun and Rudi guessed he would use it if he saw Rudi leaving with information about the killing of his brother Renko. Taking the decision to turn south towards the town of Comănești instead of risking a meeting with Tigo on the road north to Moinești, he urged the horse along at its best pace. He did not notice the stationery lorry on the road to Moinești, but Tigo looked up from watching the driver try to repair the flat tyre and saw the distinctive vardo turning onto the road south.

Pesha kept his car running almost flat out to get to Moinești as soon as he could, to pass on information about his hated oppressor. Finally arriving at the town, he stopped only to ask for directions to the police station and then drove up alongside the big building. His wife was suspicious of the police and wanted to stay in the car, but Pesha was worried that Tigo would come after him and if he saw his wife, he would either harm her, or abduct her. The two Romas hurried up the steps and their way was then blocked by a burly policeman, who wanted to know why they were in such a hurry. Tigo produced the Reward Leaflet and told him that he knew where Tigo was, but they would have to hurry if they wanted to catch him. A sergeant heard the conversation and walked over to speak with Pesha.

All police stations in the area had been alerted to the search for the murderer and instructed to telephone Lieutenant Bumbesco immediately if they received information on his whereabouts. The sergeant told Pesha to follow him to the office of his superior, but asked his wife to remain with the constable. After listening to Pesha, the police telephoned Bumbesco who was at the time driving along the country road leading to Moinești. After checking his map, he found that he was only three miles from the turn off to Pasiti and he arranged to meet with three policemen there to drive together to Pasiti. He would have liked to surround the village to prevent Tigo escaping into the forest, but one policeman had to remain in Moinești and the small town had a total force of only six and two were off duty.

Bumbesco intended to park outside Pasiti so that the car engines would not be heard and then have his team approach from four sides by walking through the surrounding forest. Pesha reluctantly agreed to go with the police team, who needed his local knowledge and they drove off to meet Bumbesco. Just short of the crossroads, they found a Roma trying to repair a tyre puncture on an old lorry. The man told them that he had been taking Tigo to Moinești to follow Pesha when the tyre made a loud noise and lost all its air. He had no spare tyre and was using useless tools and hoping to patch the hole in his inner tube. Tigo had seen Rudi turn towards Comănești and had run back to Pasiti to fetch his horse and follow him. They heard the sound of a car engine and saw Bumbesco drive up in his Suzuki.

As soon as he heard that Tigo could be riding after Rudi, Bumbesco told the policemen to drive into Pasiti as quickly as possible and if they found Tigo to arrest him, or shoot him if he tried to escape. He had just met with Rudi on his way to the crossroads and told him to park at the roadside and wait until Tigo had been captured and he would return. If Rudi had tethered the horse and was sitting near his vardo, he would make an ideal target for Tigo with his hunting rifle. Rudi had been surprised to see Bumbesco's car coming towards him and the two men had exchanged information on Tigo. The lieutenant asked him to wait at the roadside to protect his horse and vardo, while he drove off to meet with his team at Pasiti.

After making sure that his horse was amongst some good grass, Rudi followed his survival instinct and placed a stool amongst some thick shrubs to give him cover. He had a clear view of the road from Pasiti and his horse and vardo. There were six bullets in his revolver and he also took a carton of twenty-five more to protect himself if Tigo escaped the police raid and came his way. It was a pleasant afternoon and as he sat silently in his hideout, he watched as small animals scurried through the grass and bushes, ignoring him as he sat motionless. Birds suddenly flew out of the trees further along the roadside and Rudi checked that the revolver's safety catch was switched on and gripped his gun. He thought he saw a flash of colour as someone, or something moved within the forest, but parallel with the road.

Some minutes passed very slowly and there was no noise apart from the rustling of the wind drifting through the trees. Rudi found himself breathing as quietly as possible and trying to look closer into the forest. He had left the door of the vardo open and suddenly there were five shots, carefully timed and probably spaced to hit anyone exposed to the line of fire through the open door. Gun smoke drifted slowly up from a spot in the forest directly opposite the open vardo door. Tigo must have hoped that Rudi was in the vardo and that the spread of shots would take him by surprise. He switched the safety catch off and raised his gun, but held his fire until he could see his target. Rudi was waiting for Tigo to walk towards the vardo to check if his shots through the doorway had hit the unseen target, but Tigo was aware that once he left the protection of the forest, he would be fully exposed.

Tigo could not know that Rudi had a gun, but the man had noticed and admired his knife and he might not want to risk having Rudi throw it at his unguarded back. Rudi smiled as he thought about two men with guns and each not wanting to show himself to the other. He guessed that Tigo was a good twenty metres away, which for him was too far for accurate shooting with a revolver. Moving off the stool, he lay flat on the ground, aimed at the area where smoke had risen and prepared to fire as soon as Tigo emerged. A small car raced up and stopped in front of the horse. Rudi could not see Bumbesco inside and guessed he was crouching down for protection after hearing rifle shots.

Bumbesco had heard the shooting as he was driving back to the vardo to help Rudi, but after he had stopped his car, the horse continued grazing contentedly and there were no more shots and no sign of anyone. Rudi was smart and Bumbesco hoped he had avoided the shots, but Tigo could be hiding nearby until he could shoot Rudi, or Bumbesco himself. He needed to get Tigo to give his position away somehow. He pulled a tent pole from the back of the car and wrapped his green hunting coat around one end. Opening the car door carefully, he moved the pole sideways, then pushed it forward so that his coat dropped outside near his front tyre. Two loud rifle shots were fired from his left immediately. One ripped through his coat and the other struck his front tyre and Bumbesco could hear the air escaping and hoped his spare was intact. At the same time, six lighter shots were fired from another part of the forest and he guessed they were from Rudi's revolver. There was a yell as someone was hit and he saw movement in the trees to his left. Pushing his rifle through the open window, he aimed at the spot and fired all ten bullets in the magazine and thought he heard another yell.

Next, he heard the sound of a horse galloping away through the forest and guessed that Tigo was escaping. He shouted out to ask Rudi if he was safe and the big Roma replied that he was and wondered if he dared leave his hiding place. Bumbesco ran into the forest behind the vardo and made his way round to Rudi by following the sound of his voice. Rudi was lying flat on the ground and explained about the shots at the inside of the vardo and that he had waited for a target, but lay down to avoid likely return fire.

"When you tempted him to fire at your car, I saw the smoke and emptied my revolver into the bushes around it. I think I hit him and when you fired all those shots, I think he was hit again."

Bumbesco suggested they split up and approach the spot where Tigo's gun smoke had shown, by coming at it from different directions. They moved warily and then found drops of blood on some leaves and the grass below where Tigo must have been hiding. It would be unwise to follow the trail through the forest themselves, but Bumbesco telephoned to call up armed men and dogs, as well as an armed policeman to travel to the vardo. The policeman would remain until transport could be arranged for the cart and horse to return to Budapest. They replaced the flat tyre with the spare and drove to Pasiti to examine Tigo's belongings and look for any likely locations where he might have gone.

Pesha was waiting with the policemen outside Tigo's house and he rushed over to Rudi and hugged him.

"Thank you, my friend, for driving that monster away from us. Now we can live without having him take our food and threaten us every day. Will I get the big reward written on the paper you gave me?"

Rudi smiled at the man, who may well have saved his life and pointed to the policeman standing beside him.

"My lieutenant is the man you should speak to and I know he has many questions also about what happened in Budestin."

Pesha gave him a detailed account of his race to Moineşti and his meeting at the police station and how he had persuaded the sergeant to hurry to Pasiti to capture the dangerous man. Bumbesco assured him that he would recommend that he should be paid something, but since Tigo had escaped, he would not receive the full amount.

"Tell me what you can remember about Budestin and how the man Renko was killed there."

"Two Romas came from France where Renko had killed the son of their chief and then another Roma came with a big Englishman and a Hungarian, who said Renko had killed his

122

sister. The French Roma wanted to kill Renko and the Hungarian wanted to take him back to Hungary for a trial. Tigo and Renko were brothers, but did not like each other. Tigo held a trial and the visitors told about how Renko had murdered their people. Tigo decided that because Renko had accepted traditional Roma hospitality in France and then killed the chief's son, it was a double crime and they should be allowed to do what they wanted to Renko. They took off his clothes and nailed his hands to a board, then left him in the forest all night. I had a bad stomach and got up in the night because my ass was on fire. When I was coming back from the forest, I heard voices and saw Tigo talking to Renko. As I passed, I heard Renko ask Tigo to do something for him and he would tell him where to find his treasure."

"What was it that Tigo promised to do?"

"I did not hear, because I was hiding and did not want Tigo to see me and beat me."

"So how did Renko die?"

"The next morning, the women gathered around Renko and taunted him and he shouted at them, which was not wise because he had raped some of the young girls. They heated their knives in the fire and then pressed them on his dick and legs. The Hungarian asked Tigo to stop them and one of the French Roma walked over and slit Renko's throat."

Bumbesco thought about this for a few minutes and decided that Renko had got what he deserved, but had paid a high price for his crimes. With the French Roma, the Englishman and the Hungarian involved, as well as the Romanian Tigo, it would be a very complicated case to try in a Romanian court and he doubted that it would proceed.

"Tell me about the stranger who came before the soldiers visited Budestin for the first time."

"He was a quiet man, but he was a friend with Tigo and taught him how to shoot his new rifle and they went away together before the soldiers came."

"You told Rudi that Tigo bought the gun with money taken from Renko's house after his brother was killed. How do you know that this is so?"

"I heard Renko tell Tigo where his treasure was and after he was killed, Tigo took his house and everything in it."

Bumbesco now had a clear report of what had happened and he thanked Pesha for his cooperation. He then asked a colleague to drive the Roma back to Moineşti to collect his wife, who had been left at the police station.

At the village there was no sympathy shown for Tigo and the police were guarding his house and waiting for Bumbesco to begin his search. Tigo was obviously very unpopular and the villagers were happy to respond to any questions about his habits and background. When asked about the visitor to their village at Budestin before the soldier's visit, a number confirmed that the man had been friendly with Tigo. He had taught him how to fire the rifle he had bought with the money he took from his brother Renko's home. Tigo's house was dirty and untidy, but hidden amongst the clutter were boxes of papers, which would take some time to examine.

Obviously Tigo had been desperate to catch and kill Pesha and Rudi because he wanted to prevent them passing on details about Renko's death. As a result of his desperate hurry to chase after the two men, he had no time to hide, or destroy the papers, which Bumbesco now collected for examination. They would all be taken back to police headquarters at Bucharest, since much of the detail was written in Hungarian. Bumbesco had some knowledge of the language, but not enough to fully understand what was written in the papers. Turning to Rudi, he complimented him for using Pesha to get his message to the police. He would do all he could to have Rudi given some worthwhile recognition, or share in the reward money for his dangerous role in Tigo's exposure. He offered to take Rudi with him on his drive back to Bucharest, but the big man wanted to stay with the vardo and be sure it was safely loaded for its return to his father. Rudi dreaded looking inside to find what damage had been done by Tigo's bullets, but was sure he would be able to make repairs before returning the vardo to his father.

After the long drive to the capital, Bumbesco tumbled into bed at his parents' home and slept until mid-morning, before presenting himself at the office of Major Chisca. The police team with dogs had followed the trail left by Tigo through the forest and discovered that their quarry had circled round and returned to Pasiti, where policemen were guarding his house. The man was either bold, or desperate to take such a risk. The dogs followed the trail to a woman's house and when they searched it, they found bloody clothes, which she had used on Tigo's wounds. Under threat of prison, she told them that Tigo had a shallow wound in his leg and a more serious wound to his shoulder. He could ride his horse, but would not be able to walk any distance. As soon as she had applied the bandages, he rode off before the dogs and men caught up with him, or someone saw him in the village and told the police. He had plenty of money and had paid her for helping him.

Chisca congratulated Bumbesco on flushing out the killer and almost capturing him. The man had been lucky and he was relieved that no one else had been injured, or killed at the shootout. A fluent Hungarian-speaking policeman joined them and they spent the rest of the day slowly working through the mass of papers. The elder brother Renko had been topping up a number of bank accounts in Hungary and Romania, as well as keeping cash at his house in Budestin. Tigo must have already collected the money from Budestin, but Chisca would arrange to have the Romanian bank accounts blocked to prevent Tigo obtaining any more money.

There were pages of details about the Pusztai family lands and property at Dunakeszi outside Budapest. Renko was trying to kill the entire family and he had forged evidence to have the father, Istvan, imprisoned and then arranged his death. Chisca had copies of the extradition request from Hungary and it described the killing of Arianne Pusztai and her husband, as well as a French citizen by the renegade Renko. There were also details of three attempts to kill the brother Demeter, who was now controlling a large aluminium mining company and living at the family home in Dunakeszi. Renko also listed documents proving the guilt of a number of senior Hungarian politicians and officials. In addition to the documents found at Pasiti, he discovered there were more in his stepbrother's home in Dunakeszi.

Having read all the papers, the men took a coffee break and discussed what Tigo was likely to do now that he was no longer a Roma chief and was a wanted fugitive in Romania. Bumbesco was the first to make a suggestion.

"Tigo made a friend of Gunari, the Roma soldier who was sent to investigate Renko's killing and he taught Tigo to shoot.

He may be the only friend that Tigo has left, but we still have no idea where he is now. My guess is that if Gunari is still alive and if we can find him, we might also find Tigo."

"You think Tigo might have killed him, perhaps because he did his job by being friendly and finding out about Renko's murder?"

"Well sir, it has to be a possibility and we know that neither of them was at Budestin for either of the visits by our soldiers. There is also the strong link to the Pusztai family. Renko killed the father and sister and we know the brother was at Budestin when Renko was killed. Will you be sending a report to the Hungarians and include the record of crimes by some of their officials?"

"It is not my decision, but I will recommend that we pass on all information regarding Hungarian subjects to their government."

Chapter 22
Confirmation

Demeter and Jack drove to the Roma village and Boldo met them outside his house and took the two men inside for the meeting with Gunari. At previous meetings, the Romanian had shown no emotion, but when he saw them, his face broke into a smile and Demeter hoped that it was a good sign. After shaking hands, the four men sat around a table and Gunari waited for the visitors to open the conversation. Demeter spoke first.

"Good morning, Gunari. I have lived here for most of my life and although my family was persecuted by the police chief Renko Veres, I believe I have many friends with the local Roma people. Unfortunately, Commissar Radics has done his best to cause trouble with your people, but you led them well in holding up production and took care to avoid injury to the workers. Your surprise evacuation of the people of the village was clever, since it protected them from possible reprisals by Radics."

The Romanian smiled and nodded his head before replying to Demeter.

"Boldo was very worried when he heard rumours that a rail line would have to be built and knew the shortest way from the mine to the refinery was through the middle of his village. I agreed to help him persuade you to move it and pass outside the village instead. When we met, I was sure that you also wanted this, but the bad man Radics hated us and tried to destroy us. I was glad sir that you stopped the line outside and then built around the village."

Demeter was relieved that Gunari did not blame him for the lack of concern about the Roma and possible destruction of their community. He tried to reassure Gunari and obtain answers.

"I hope now that we can live together as friends and there will be work for those who want it. I must ask you Gunari if you know anyone who would want to harm me, or my fiancée, because someone fired a shot at her when she was riding near my home. The bullet missed her, but killed her horse and it is possible that whoever fired was actually aiming at me and missed."

Gunari looked genuinely surprised to hear about the shooting at Dunakeszi and the men watched his facial expressions as he seemed to be considering possibilities before giving a reply.

"Killing always brings more killing and I am glad your lady was not harmed. I have a friend in Romania and he is the brother of this Renko who hated your family and tried to kill all of you. The brother does not know you and has no reason to harm you. We spent some weeks together in the mountains and I taught him to shoot a rifle he had bought. Then we came here together and he visited his brother's family house, but he stayed only two days then returned to his people, where he was chief."

"Where did you learn your shooting skill, Gunari?"

"I was for eight years in the army and there I did much extra training and always I was the best."

"My friend thought that you might have had military training, like him. Is this friend called Tigo?"

Gunari nodded his head and Demeter looked at Jack, who frowned and waved his hand to indicate that Demeter should go on with his questions about Tigo.

"Could Tigo have returned here without you knowing and fired his rifle at me?"

"If he returned, he would surely come to see me and I was here when you were attacked, but I did not meet with him."

"We have met Tigo and we know that he is a violent man, unlike you. We were at Tigo's village when he agreed to have two Roma crucify his brother and we could see that he hated his older brother."

"He did not tell me you were there, but said his brother had killed the son of a Roma chief after taking their food and a bed. Two men came and killed him on the orders of the chief and Tigo was afraid to stop them."

Jack spoke in English to Demeter to tell him that Gunari had been told part of the truth by Tigo, who could well be the shooter.

"We know what really happened in Romania and you have not been told the truth. Tigo decided that his brother should be given to the two French Roma, who then crucified him before killing him. With his older brother dead, he was no longer a threat to Tigo as the chief and he could take his brother's treasures. When you went to the mountains with Tigo and taught him to shoot, did you teach him other things which you learned as a soldier?"

Gunari shook his head and appeared surprised that he had been misled by his friend and explained why he had helped Tigo.

"I was a good soldier and always was first in the special training classes, but others who were not good were promoted and I was not because I am a Roma. I was sent to Budestin to find out if a report by some Hungarians about a killing were true. Tigo welcomed me and it was good to be among my people again and I decided to use my training to help them. Tigo wanted very much to learn all he could from me and when we were together in the forest, I taught him to prepare and to plan instead of acting with anger, or fear. He said nothing about your family, or Hungary, but I think now he was more clever than I thought. He took advantage of my goodwill towards our people to learn what would help him to get what he wanted."

Demeter thanked Gunari for his honesty and he and Jack drove back to the refinery office, where an unexpected visitor was waiting for them. Jack recognised the senior policeman immediately from their last meeting at Demeter's mansion, after he had wounded two would be assassins.

"It's good to see you again Major Herceg, but I assure you that I have not shot any of your countrymen since we last met."

With a smile on his face the policeman nodded his head and responded.

"It is now Colonel, since you two gentlemen helped to expose Commissar Radics, who has now been replaced by my boss and I am his deputy. When we last met, I congratulated you on wounding the two Roma in police uniforms, who attacked my men and tried to kill you Demeter. Once again, I am in your debt and perhaps, now I can repay you with some information."

Demeter was surprised that the senior policeman had travelled from Budapest to talk to them and was first to respond.

"Our congratulations to you Colonel, and it is always a pleasure to meet you."

Herceg acknowledged the cordial greeting and congratulations by giving Demeter a short bow and a beaming smile, before explaining the purpose of his visit.

"Yesterday, I had a visit at Police HQ in Budapest from two Romanian police officers, Major Chisca and Lieutenant Bumbesco. There were two very brutal murders in Romania when a police commissar and a soldier were killed. Bumbesco is obviously a very clever man and he traced the murderer to a small Roma village called Budestin. A Hungarian called Renko Veres was killed there and you two gentlemen were present when this happened. You returned to Hungary and reported the incident and Commissar Radics had already requested that the Romanians extradite Veres, because he had killed your sister and others. After Radics read your report that Veres was dead, he wrote to the Romanian authorities with the information and cancelled his earlier request for the extradition of the man, Veres. Commissar Dalca decided that soldiers should be sent to Budestin and one was killed, as well as a young boy and the mother of the chief when the village itself was destroyed. It was Tigo, the chief of Budestin who then murdered the Romanian commissar and soldier in revenge.

"Bumbesco shot and wounded Tigo and nearly captured him, but he escaped into the forest on a horse. The Romanians found a mass of documents in Tigo's house, which he had gathered from his brother and they incriminate some of our own government officials. They are now being investigated. As a result of questioning witnesses, Bumbesco also believes that Tigo made a promise to his dying brother that he would continue the vendetta against the Pusztai family. In return, he was told where Veres kept his money and documents hoard. Bumbesco is convinced that because you Demeter, reported the killing of his brother to the Hungarian authorities, his mother was killed and his village destroyed. He asked me to warn you that Tigo has money, is armed and may well come to Dunakeszi to try to kill you. Unfortunately, Tigo has been taught to shoot by a Romanian soldier, who is still missing."

Demeter and Jack saw the shock as the news registered on each other's faces and Jack asked for details of the two killings in Romania. Both men were horrified when Herceg described the hanging from a tree and burial alive. Jack was first to speculate on a possible link at Dunakeszi.

"Demeter was riding with his fiancée and her horse was shot dead. I wondered if it was a bad miss and Demeter was the actual target, but now we know he probably was. Tigo could well have been the shooter. We have just been speaking to a Romanian ex-soldier named Gunari, who admits to having taught Tigo to shoot and he is probably the missing Romanian soldier that Bumbesco mentioned to you."

"It seems that Bumbesco was right and Demeter and possibly you Jack are now top of his revenge list. We don't know how serious his wounds are, but he will need time to recover before making his way to Hungary. Tigo was shot in a Romanian forest six weeks ago and if he intends to come after Demeter, he could well have made his way here and may not expect to find you here as well Jack. The Romanians will probably want to question their lost soldier, who is an army deserter. Do you know how to contact him?"

"Yes, he seems to be settling in at the local Roma village and is beginning to speak Hungarian."

Demeter had taken an immediate dislike of Tigo when they met the arrogant chief at his village and was delighted when Jack had put the bully flat on his back when he had suddenly tried to hit him. After Tigo's brother was killed, Demeter, Jack and a Roma from Dunakeszi left the village together with the two French Roma and Tigo seemed glad to see them go. At the time, it seemed to be the end of a trail of murders, but it had led to the start of another rash of killing.

Having warned them of the danger, Colonel Herceg was anxious to return to his new position at Budapest Police Headquarters and the men shook hands and thanked the policeman for passing on the full details of Tigo's barbaric activities in Romania. Although offered extra police help to protect them, both Demeter and Jack decided that a lone assassin was better dealt with by anticipating his actions and out thinking him. After watching the police car drive away from the office, the two friends began to plan what they needed to do to protect themselves and to make their preparations. As they shared a meal together in the evening, Demeter admitted that after fearing for his life since he was a teenager and thinking the threats had finally ended, he was shocked that it was now beginning all over again. Jack told him that between them they must either kill, or capture the renegade Romanian and finally end the vendetta on the Pusztai estate.

Chapter 23
Transformation

Tigo had been suspicious of the big man from the moment he found him with his vardo at the roadside outside his village and he now wished he had turned his rifle on him, instead of the wild boars. When the old Mercedes lorry suddenly swung to the left as the front tyre blew out, he stood alongside as the wheel was being changed. Out of the corner of his eye, he saw the vardo come to the crossing and turn south, away from the Moineşti road. Rudi was using his absence to leave Pasiti and could be going to talk to the police about him and the killing at Budestin, after that vermin Pesha blabbed about it. He had seen the reward notices in many villages and torn down every one he saw.

He would make sure that Pesha was not able to say any more when he caught him, but first he must stop Rudi. He would have to run back and collect his horse and then take the short cut through the forest to catch him. He ran all the way back to Pasiti and quickly saddled his horse before galloping off to chase after Rudi, who would only make a slow pace with the heavy vehicle. When he reached the road going south, he checked the soft surface and could find no wheel tracks, so the man had not passed. He wondered if Rudi had stopped, or turned around and gone to Moineşti instead, so riding close to the tree line he headed back towards the crossroads.

After ten minutes, he saw the vardo ahead, with the horse grazing alongside, but there was no sign of Rudi. He led his horse into the forest so that he could get closer without being seen, or heard. After tethering his horse, he moved into the trees across the road from the vardo with his loaded rifle and looked for movement. There was no noise and no sign of Rudi, but the vardo door was open and he moved quietly through the trees until he was directly opposite. Just inside he could see some sort of curtain, but nothing was moving. He waited, but there was still no movement and he was sure that Rudi must be inside the vardo, but out of sight. Remembering what he had been taught, he fired five of the six shots in the magazine, spacing them carefully to cover a wide area inside the vardo, but kept one shot to cover any movement. After the loud noise of the gunshots, silence returned and only the horse was affected as the sudden noise startled it into straining against its tether. Again, he waited with the gun reloaded and ready to fire. He was then surprised to see a small car race up and stop alongside the horse with the driver crouched down inside and out of sight. Tigo guessed that the driver must have heard the shots and was protecting himself, but why did he not just drive away, unless he too was an enemy.

Tigo aimed his gun at the car and waited. A flash of coloured movement showed just outside the car front and Tigo reacted with two shots, but then he heard bullets zipping into the trees where he was standing and one struck his shoulder. He ran into the forest for his horse and then there were more shots and he felt a blow to his upper leg. Climbing up into the saddle he rode slowly away and headed in the direction of his village. When he approached through the trees, he saw the police outside his house. He was bleeding badly and knew he must have his wounds bound before he could start making the long ride to safety.

He tethered the horse in the trees and made for old Lala's house. She had been old when he was still a teenager, but she knew the old remedies and how to make her balms and powders from plants only she recognised in the forest. When she saw him and the blood she was startled, but he covered her mouth and told her he would pay her well if she helped him. She bound his wounds and covered them with her own remedy to prevent infection. He thanked her and gave her the money he had promised, then told her he was making for Moineşti, knowing she would tell the police.

Hearing voices outside, he peered through a window and saw a tall, dark haired man standing outside in hunting clothes and speaking with two policemen outside his house. The policemen were listening carefully and saluted as the man walked into his house. Tigo had only ever seen policemen in uniform, but although the man was dressed like a hunter, he had an air of authority about him and was definitely a leader. Watching the man walk into his house, Tigo felt sick in his stomach as he realised the policeman must be going to search it. Anxious to chase after Pesha, he had left all the papers taken from his brother in a cupboard and now they would be found. His horse was tethered at the back of Lala's house, but at any moment someone might recognise it and alert the police. Waiting until the policemen had moved away, Tigo edged out of the house, untied his horse and led it into the forest.

It was painful to walk as he kept out of sight of the police and made sure he was well away from the village before mounting his horse. Being careful to try and avoid reopening his wounds, he managed to pull himself up into the saddle and ride away. His wounds hurt and he knew that his people would no longer fear, or obey him. He was now an outcast with a price on his head and every policeman in the area would be looking for him. He knew he must change his name and his appearance, but first he had to find somewhere to shelter until he regained his strength. His only hope was to ride as far as he could before the police had time to arrange a wide search, or close off the area.

After riding for over three hours through the darkness, he found it difficult to stay in the saddle and knew that soon he would have to stop. Riding out of a copse of trees, he saw ahead of him a single storey house and alongside an old barn with a sagging roof. Sliding from his horse, he edged open the wooden barn door and walked inside with his horse. There was an old plough horse in a stall and a bag of hay alongside. He managed to tether his horse and spread some hay for it to eat before collapsing onto the floor and instantly falling asleep.

As dawn broke, he was suddenly awakened by someone kicking his buttocks and as he looked up in the half light, he saw a figure above him holding a shotgun and glaring down at him. Forcing a smile, he raised his hands and slowly got to his feet as his aching body reminded him of the hours spent in the saddle. Looking at the elderly man confronting him, he offered his apologies.

"I am sorry to have used your barn, but it was late at night and I had ridden for many hours until I was too tired to ride any further. I will pay you for the hay and shelter for last night."

The man watched as Tigo took some notes from his pocket and held them out. The man cradled the gun under one arm and eagerly reaching out to take the money. Tigo quickly drew his knife and stepping forward drove it into the farmer's chest. The man dropped the gun and clutched at his wound, but his heart was pierced and he collapsed to the barn floor as he gave out his last breath. Tigo wiped his knife on the farmer's shirt, picked up the money and shotgun, checked it and was surprised to find there were no cartridges in the barrels. He dropped it on the hay and picked up his own gun before making his way to the farmhouse to check if there was anyone else inside.

The door was partly open and Tigo moved carefully into the large kitchen with his gun ready to fire, but there was no one in the house and Tigo knew that he had found his haven. He would be able to hide here and give his wounds time to mend before leaving Romania and joining up with Gunari in Hungary. There were chickens outside in the yard, which should give him eggs and he knew many ways to cook a chicken. He also found flour, coffee and some other bagged food in a cupboard. His last meal had been breakfast, which he had the day before when he drove off after Pesha. His stomach was now so empty it was aching and he went out to the yard and caught a chicken. After wringing its neck and plucking the feathers, he was soon roasting it over a fire in the kitchen range.

After the hot chicken meal and some coffee, he felt stronger and even lost some of the pain after his night ride. It also helped to bolster his determination to escape to a new life well away from Romania. He knew he had first to bury the farmer and then explore the farm and buildings to make sure it was safe to use for the week, or so, before he was fit enough to move on. He dug out a patch of long grass and after laying the thick turf to one side, prepared a grave for the farmer in the earth beneath. The man was heavy and Tigo was not yet strong enough to lift him to his shoulder and instead had to drag the body from the barn. After toppling it into the grave, he threw earth on top until it was level and stamped the surface down with his boots. His last job was to carefully replace the long grass turf and water it in. Within days the grass would have recovered and would blend in with the rest of the area so that there would be no sign of the grave.

After spending an hour walking around the fields and buildings, Tigo could find no livestock, apart from the plough horse and knew the farmer had grown only arable crops. He led both horses out of the barn and left them to feed on the grass in a meadow behind the house. There was also a field of potatoes and he dug up a good supply and laid them out to dry in the yard. They should provide him with meals for a week, or more. On a shelf in the kitchen he found a pack of twenty-five 12-bore cartridges for the shotgun, which he would be able to use to shoot rabbits and supplement his food supply. He was relieved that he had found shelter and enough food to sustain him until his wounds healed.

Searching the rooms, he discovered letters and other papers in a drawer, which showed that the famer's name was Corel Borel and he seemed to be living alone. There was also an old and badly creased National Identity Card showing a younger Corel Borel. At the bottom of another drawer were photographs of the farmer with a woman alongside, but Tigo thought she could have died, or left the man. He also found letters from a Borel family living in Bistrita. If there were any callers, he would have to convince them that he was looking after the farm for Borel, who was visiting relatives in Bistrita. If they became suspicious, he could always dig another grave.

Exercise would help him to regain his strength and he did some work around the farm each morning. Tigani people were adept at make do and mend and he repaired the barn door and farmhouse porch, as well as weeding the potato field. Cleaning the windows and sweeping and tidying up the house altered the appearance of neglect that previously dominated. A week passed and he had shaved off his beard and cut his long hair so short that he could feel the cold air on his scalp. Having been previously shielded from the sun by his thick beard and shoulder length hair, his chin and neck were pale compared to the rest of his face. By sitting with his head tilted towards the sun each day, he was slowly getting more colour on his face and head. He needed to hide having removed his beard and long hair. He was trying to make himself look more like the photograph of Corel Borel on the farmer's National Identity Card after bending it so that one of the creases made the year of birth too hard to read.

Soon, he would be able to continue his journey towards the Hungarian border on his way to meet up with his friend Gunari and pass himself off as Corel Borel. There was no coffee, or sugar left and with the larder empty he had to rely on what he could grow, or shoot. He had no future here in Romania anymore, but together the two of them could start new lives by making sure there were no Pusztai family left. It would give him a claim on their land as well as revenge for the death of his mother and destruction of his village.

On his last visit to Dunakeszi, he had crossed the border into Hungary near Satu Mare, but Gunari had chosen the bus routes and bought the tickets for him. While Gunari was holding meetings with the Tigani in the area, he had been exploring the land and dreaming of the day when he would be able to settle here with his own people and take advantage of the money and secret information hidden by his half-brother Renko. He had also been able to find some of the papers his brother Renko had hidden in the village.

He was nervous about travelling by bus, or train as a wanted man and was going to make the long ride to Dunakeszi by horse and try to stay on woodland trails. He would be carrying food, the rifle and shotgun and was hoping to buy food and shoot more rabbits during the journey. There would be Tigani camps along the way and he should be able to make use of them once he had changed his appearance. He had only twelve rounds for his rifle in his cartridge belt, but might be able to buy more along the way.

During his long ride through the forest he had been able to use his good arm to hold the reins and protect his throbbing left shoulder. Although his leg injury was not as deep, the riding movement had opened the wound and he knew he had lost quite a lot of blood. After two weeks hiding and recovering on the farm, he still felt stiff and sore and realised that his strength had not yet recovered enough for the ride across the country to reach Hungary. He knew his life in Romania was finished, but he hoped he could start a new life in Hungary. He also wondered if his luck would hold so that he could spend another week recovering and relaxing at the farm. He had been shooting rabbits to avoid killing more chickens, since they were giving him a good supply of eggs. He was in the kitchen cleaning the two guns when he heard the sound of an engine and looking through the window, he watched as a large van stopped outside and a man stepped out and began walking towards the kitchen door.

Chapter 24
Revelation

After the worrying news from Colonel Herceg, Jack insisted that they should arm themselves and as well as the old hunting rifle which Demeter used, they bought two automatic hand guns and Jack chose an automatic rifle with a ten-round magazine and a scope. When they tested their guns on some made up targets behind the house, Jack was relieved to find that Demeter was quite a good shot and he himself had undergone sniper training with the army. They should be able to defend themselves in a shootout, but Jack knew that it would be almost impossible to protect themselves from a hidden marksman choosing a moment when one of them was exposed. Having already extended his stay in Hungary, Jack needed to return home to be with his family and take care of his business, but he was concerned about leaving Demeter in danger and agreed to return as soon as possible.

Jack suggested that if Tigo was wounded and being hunted by the Romanian police, it could be at least three weeks before he was likely to recover. Then it could take him another two weeks, or three to make his way across Romania to Dunakeszi. He planned to return from Liverpool to be with Demeter in three weeks' time, but if there were signs that Tigo was in the area, he would fly back as soon as possible. The two men spoke with Janos about the threat and offered him a handgun. As he worked around the mansion, he could be a target, but by carrying the automatic at all times, he would be able to defend himself. Janos had never fired a gun before and Jack gave him instructions in loading, aiming and firing. After finally persuading Janos not to close his eyes when pulling the trigger and then emptying the magazine, Jack finally managed to get him aiming the gun before firing. He was unlikely to hit anything more than five metres away, but his wild shooting would probably scare an assassin as much as it did Jack.

The rifles were kept loaded, with one stored in a cloakroom near the front entrance and the other in a kitchen cupboard at the rear of the house. If there was an attack on the house from the outside, it should be possible to get to one of the rifles quickly and confront the attacker. If the intruder managed to get inside the house, the handguns carried by Demeter and Janos would be more effective in the confined space.

After Jack had flown home to Liverpool, Demeter was kept busy at the mine and when he returned home each night, he made sure that the doors and shutters on the ground floor windows were locked. As the days passed with no signs of an attack by Tigo, he began to hope that after being shot by the Romanian police, the killer had given up on his murderous plan for revenge and hidden himself away somewhere in the wild countryside. Demeter warned Janos not to begin taking chances with their strict security regime until they were sure that the threat from Tigo had positively been removed.

At home in Liverpool, Jack made an early start at his office to clear the back load of queries built up during his extended stay in Hungary. He was pleased to find that the mail order business was showing steady growth and made a note to compliment the manager on his good work. The shootout with the Russian Mafia had removed the threat to his security staff and with his business again running smoothly, he should be able to spend more time with the family. Unfortunately, he could not forget the threat to his friend Demeter and made regular telephone calls to ask if there was as yet any sign of Tigo in the Dunakeszi area. Theresa had returned to Durham University with her right arm in plaster, since she was left-handed and would be able to continue making notes during her lectures.

Amongst the papers on his desk was a note that 'a friend' had called three times and although he would not leave his name, he insisted that it was essential that he speak with Jack as soon as he returned from Hungary. Jack waited until nine o'clock before dialling the number he had been given. A muffled voice said, "Hello," but without giving a name and the speaker was obviously waiting for Jack to introduce himself.

141

"My name is Jack Randil and I have a note asking me to ring this number."

"Oh it's you Jack. Thank God you called. It's Gary Dempsey. I was afraid to leave my name because I dare not run the risk of Don Taylor finding out I had contacted your office. I can't use my house phone, but bought a cheap pay as you go for this number."

"I thought Don Taylor was very pleased with you for risking your life to protect his money. What did you do to make him turn nasty towards you?"

"I told him that I'd had enough and wanted to retire and leave Liverpool with my family to make a new life. He said my family was free to go anytime, but I had too much information in my head and he needed me to help him to run the business until he was ready to retire. He suggested I stay working for him until his retirement, or I could shoot myself, or he would do it for me."

"So what do you want me for?"

"I can give your police friends all the information they need to put Don Taylor away for life and close down the Young Guns operations in the city. If I give them this, I need police protection for me and my family and relocation for us with new names under their Witness Protection Scheme. It must be done quickly, before Don decides I am now too much of a risk."

"So you want me to be the go between for you and the family."

"I trust you Jack, and know you are smart enough to pull it off. Will you help us?"

"Right, say or do nothing until I ring this number tomorrow at this time."

"Oh thank you Jack, you can't know how grateful I am for that, I will be waiting for your call. I just knew you would help me."

After putting his phone down, Jack sat at his desk thinking about his conversation with Gary and wondering why he kept getting involved in other people's problems, however much he tried to concentrate on his own family and business. Remembering the many times he had just missed death, he realised he had been lucky so far, but others needed his luck and help as well. He telephoned through to his friend Peter at

Liverpool CID and told him about the conversation he had just had with Gary.

"We've been trying to put Taylor away for years Jack, and now you come up with an offer of inside help. I will speak with the super and get back to you quickly. We can't afford to foul up on this chance, or get Gary killed."

Although he knew that the police would make all the necessary arrangements, Jack could not stop his mind from working out the safest method of collecting Gary and his family without raising the suspicions of the watchers. His house would be under constant surveillance by the Young Guns and any visit would have to look natural, but produce a quick and safe escape for the family. It was essential that the gang had no suspicions, which would prompt them to destroy evidence, or close down their operations before the police could act. As he waited for a response from Peter, he tried to concentrate on his business correspondence, but found it impossible to clear thoughts of Gary from his mind. Just over half an hour later the phone rang. Peter confirmed that his super was keen to meet with Gary and agree to his requests in return for evidence to convict Don Taylor and the Young Guns gang.

"Just a minute Jack, my boss wants to speak to you and I will put you through to him."

As he waited for the connection, an idea suddenly crossed his mind and Jack found himself considering a simple scheme to collect Gary and his family without raising too many suspicions by any watchers. The Superintendent greeted him and he responded.

"Hi Larry. It's a relief to hear you might be able to help Gary and get the Young Guns off our streets. The man is overweight and middle aged and has certainly suffered a lot of stress, particularly during recent months. He is an ideal candidate for a heart attack, which would then mean he would have to be taken to hospital by ambulance. His wife and daughter could travel with him and if he is being watched, it would appear to be a normal family emergency. A watcher could not be sure whether or not it was a genuine emergency and would probably contact Taylor, but that would give us time to have Gary safely delivered to the hospital and tucked away in intensive care."

"Why we haven't recruited you for the force just amazes me Jack. That sounds like a great idea. Let me make the necessary arrangements and then I will give you a number for his wife to ring and put things in motion. Try to agree a 10 am collection time with Gary so that I can prepare the hospital telephone operator to respond on that number. We will have to put a couple of armed police in the ambulance in case of trouble and I will also have armed back up in the area to give support, just in case it's needed."

"Thanks Larry. I promised Gary I would ring him tomorrow, so let's hope he stays indoors and Taylor doesn't decide to protect himself by having Gary killed tonight. I will ring him at 8:30 am and tell him what we have in mind and if he agrees, he must explain the plan to his wife, so that she can make the emergency call."

After the evening meal, Jack told his wife about the telephone call from Gary and his plan to take Gary and his family out of their house by using an ambulance. When she heard that Jack was again getting involved with the vicious gang run by Taylor, Judy felt the fear rising from her stomach at the thought of possible harm to her husband.

"Please don't take any risks with those monsters Jack. If they find that you helped Gary, they will kill you and you have to think about me and the children. We need you too."

"I will just make the phone call and tell Gary what to do and the police will do the rest. Only the police know that Gary has contacted me."

A thunderstorm during the night woke the children and Judy had to shake Jack to wake him from his usual deep sleep. He helped her with drinks and to calm the children down. When they finally returned to bed, neither Jack, nor his wife could get back to sleep and he was at his office a good hour before his usual starting time.

He wrote down the points he wanted to cover so that Gary and his wife would be able to convince any watchers that it was a genuine heart attack. At 8:30 am he rang the mobile number Gary had given him and after a long wait he heard a hoarse whispered voice on the line.

"Wha', who's that?"

"You spoke to me yesterday and I promised to ring you back on this number."

"Oh Jack, I can't take any chances because I am scared to death, but I can't stand it any longer and you are my only hope."

Jack told Gary about his discussion with the police and the plan to have Gary and his family taken to Walton Hospital in an ambulance. There was a silence as Gary considered the offer and then agreed to do whatever was needed to escape from his dependence on the Young Guns. After going over the plan twice, Jack was satisfied that Gary would be able to have his wife make the emergency call at 10 am, follow the stretcher holding her husband and climb into the ambulance with their daughter. Satisfied that he had completed the arrangements with Gary, he then telephoned Peter to confirm that they should be ready for the call and pick up the family.

It took an effort to direct his mind back to running the business and as Judy had insisted, allow the police to take control of all contacts with Gary. Since Judy should now have taken the boys to their school, he telephoned to tell her that his involvement with the Young Guns accountant was now finished. Judy was full of praise and relief that he was keeping his promise. Ten minutes later his heart sank as he received another phone call from Gary, who was almost incoherent with worry.

Gary had carefully written down the details as Jack briefed him on the ambulance pick up, since he did not want to ruin his only chance of surviving. Slipping his mobile phone into his pocket he turned to his wife and carefully explained her role. Daughter Rosanne was not an early riser and after her frightening experience when she was abducted by the Russians, she spent much of her time in her room and delayed going back to university.

In recent weeks, she had been showing extreme mood swings and the couple were hoping that a break away from Liverpool would help her to regain her old confidence. Arm in arm on the settee, they waited in a tense state as time passed and just before 10 am, Gary passed the landline telephone to his wife. He again stressed that she must make herself sound frightened when speaking to the hospital receptionist. Her call was transferred immediately and a male voice asked her to describe her husband's symptoms, before reassuring her that an ambulance would be sent.

Gary packed money, cheques and copies of the Young Guns bank account and operating details in a small bag and asked his wife to go to Rosanne and explain her role. Two minutes later, Mary burst into the lounge with frightened eyes and quivering lips.

"She isn't there. Her bed has been made up with pillows and her bedroom is empty. Oh Gary, where can she be? Could those terrible people have got her again?"

Gary held his head in his hands as he tried to think what to do about losing his daughter for the second time. Taylor knew nothing about his contact with Jack Randil and he had accepted the man's ultimatum to continue working as his accountant. He rang Jack Randil, who picked up his phone and was startled to hear Gary's voice as he blurted out the news about his missing daughter. When he heard about the pillows in her bed, he guessed that the girl had gone out with friends.

"The ambulance will be with you within minutes Gary, so keep to the plan and let the police search for Rosanne. She has probably spent the night with her boyfriend, or girlfriends. Once you and your wife are safe, the police can concentrate their resources on finding her, but I am sure she will be back. I will speak to my police contact and tell him she is missing, but I don't believe she has been taken by Taylor."

Jack passed on the news about the missing girl to Peter Kershaw, who was relieved to hear that Jack had persuaded the accountant to go ahead with the ambulance pick up and leave the police to search for his daughter. Peter contacted his men who were watching the house and was relieved to hear that the ambulance, with Gary and his wife inside, had just left. Although he had yet to be informed, her father would not be seeing his daughter alive ever again.

Don Taylor had seen the change in Gary after the terrifying visit by the Russians and his daughter's kidnapping. The man had saved his money and been a loyal worker for many years, but could now be a possible threat to him and gang operations. After the meeting with Gary, when he insisted that his accountant must carry on, he decided he must keep a careful watch on him. Knowing that Roseanne was vulnerable because of her over protective parents, he arranged to have a good-looking young gang member become friendly with her and keep him informed of any possible threats to him. Don himself had no head for figures, but needed time to find a suitable replacement before dealing with Gary.

After her terrifying experiences, the young Roseanne rarely went outside the house at night and she was depressed and vulnerable. She quickly formed a strong attachment to the good-looking charmer she met in a coffee bar during an afternoon visit with friends. Each night, after telling her mother that she wanted to read in her room, she used pillows to make her bed look as if she was sleeping, knowing her mother would not switch on the light and disturb her sleep. After first checking that her parents were in bed, she telephoned Carl to pick her up in his BMW coupe and take her out to Liverpool nightclubs. After a hot and noisy evening with Carl and having tried some of the little pills he offered her, Rosanne was in high spirits with her arms wrapped around Carl when the police raided the club.

Carl was well known to the police and about to be handcuffed, when Rosanne reached inside his jacket for his gun. She then held it with both hands to threaten the police and run from the club with her boyfriend. Seeing a wild-eyed young girl holding an automatic, the crowds and police wisely kept back as the couple ran to their car and drove off. An alert was immediately put out and an armed response unit was soon following the BMW as it raced through the Liverpool outskirts at over eighty miles an hour. Anxious to lose the flashing blue lights behind him, Carl entered a roundabout too fast, lost control and crashed head on into the rear of a heavy lorry. The entire front of the BMW was crushed and when the emergency services arrived, the car had to be cut open before the lifeless bodies inside could be removed. Carl was quickly identified, but his female companion carried no money, credit cards or anything showing her name. Neither the driver nor the passenger had been wearing seatbelts.

Chapter 25
Payback

A small group of hospital staff had been briefed on the need to make Gary look as if his life was in danger and after first being taken to the Intensive Care Ward, he was then moved to a private room with his wife. The hospital receptionist was told to report his condition as serious to any callers, which should help to prevent Don Taylor making any rash moves. Police security was also stepped up to protect Gary. He refused to pass over documents or any information about the Young Guns until the police had found Roseanne and she had joined her parents. The previous night he had spent hours changing passwords and transferring funds so that Don Taylor could not access the money earned by his criminal activities.

It was mid-afternoon before Jack Randil and Inspector Peter Kilshaw visited Gary. His wife had returned home with a discreet police escort so that she could collect clothes and other items and because she hoped that Roseanne had returned. As he looked at their serious faces, Gary immediately guessed that they had come with bad news about his daughter. When Jack placed a gold bracelet in his hands, Gary groaned as he recognised it as Roseanne's. With tears filling his eyes he looked up at Jack.

"She never had a chance after I was tempted to work for Don Taylor and now by trying to save myself it has cost her life. Tell me what has happened."

Jack explained his daughter's evening outings with the Young Guns man and the nightclub confrontation the previous evening, the reckless driving during the pursuit followed by the fatal car crash. Gary had more questions, but was relieved to hear that because neither of the occupants in the car were wearing seatbelts, their death would have been instantaneous with such a collision at high speed. After identifying Carl as the car driver, the police wondered if his teenage girlfriend was Roseanne Dempsey and were hoping that the bracelet would help her father to make the identification.

"That devil Taylor only cared about himself and even Roseanne wasn't safe from his killer's hands. I will help you all I can, just so long as that monster gets what's coming to him. I always knew that one day I would need some sort of insurance to protect myself and for the past four years I have kept records and evidence. I hid the gun he used to kill one of the Russians at my house after he gave it to me to destroy in the big furnace in my cellar. It should have his prints on it. I want him and all the gang put away where they won't harm ordinary people anymore. You will find papers and diaries with names and places in this holdall and the gun and other evidence is hidden in my attic."

After looking through the documents that Gary had carefully accumulated over the past five years, Peter realised that they had more than enough to prove Taylor's guilt in crimes and killings. He rang his boss to give him a broad outline and the Superintendent immediately arranged for teams of armed officers to arrest Taylor and his criminal colleagues throughout the city. Finally, the police should be able to close down the biggest gang in the city. Peter put his arm around Jack's shoulders and thanked his friend for helping to make it possible. After shaking hands with Gary and sympathising with him over the loss of his daughter Jack made his way home. He could now reassure his wife that he had kept his promise by keeping his involvement to a minimum and allowing the police to deal with the gang. Judy was relieved to hear that Taylor would be locked up until his trial, but tears trickled down her cheeks as Jack described the violent death of Roseanne Dempsey.

He had told Demeter that he would return to Dunakeszi in three weeks, or sooner, if there were any more attacks on the mine, or any signs that Tigo was in the area. Until his help was needed, he would look after his family and his growing business. When he accepted his appointment to the Hun-Al board, he had no idea that it would take up so much of his time. In addition to his work in Hun-Al, there had been constant sabotage against the company and he also had to protect Demeter and himself from life threatening attacks. With the Liverpool situation finally returning to normal, he could only hope that during the coming weeks he would also see the end of the long running vendetta against the Pustaszi family. Over the years it had resulted in many deaths, but with the Romanian and Hungarian police looking for the main suspect Tigo, the man would have to be very lucky, or resourceful to evade capture. Until the family feud was ended, he would continue do his best to prevent Theresa returning to Hungary, where her life would be in danger. Now that his niece was safely in Durham, he hoped that he and Demeter could work with the police to capture Tigo.

Judy wanted her husband to give up the Hun-Al involvement and spend more time in Liverpool with her and the children. Concerned about the strength of her feelings, he gave her his word that the coming visit to Hungary would be his last as a director of Hun-Al. He was determined to help the police put Tigo in prison, so that Demeter and Theresa could marry and settle down to a normal life in Dunakeszi. He would then be able to spend all his time with his own family in Liverpool.

Chapter 26
Destination

After seeing no other people anywhere near the farm area since he first hid in the barn, Tigo was startled to see a man walk towards the open door of the farmhouse kitchen. His natural cunning had already allowed him to make up a plausible reason for his presence at the farm. Once he had learned who the man was and why he was calling, he would decide whether or not he should kill him. If the man appeared suspicious, he would have to kill him. Tigo stood in the kitchen doorway waiting and as he approached, the man smiled and called out a greeting.

The two men shook hands and noticing the stranger looking around the yard, Tigo told him that he was working for the farmer, Corel Borel to help to tidy up the buildings and fields while the farmer was visiting family near Bistrita. The man nodded and introduced himself.

"My name is Nicu and I call here whenever I am in the area to sell groceries and many other things because the people here are very far from stores. I have noticed that old Borel has not bothered much about the place for a while now, but I can see that you have repaired this porch to stop it from falling down. The potato field looks healthy too and you should have a good crop. How long will Borel be away?"

"My name is Renko and I agreed to stay for a month only because I want to visit family in Arad. I promised Borel I would do this, but warned him that if he has not returned by then, I will have to lock the place up and ride on. The chickens and the old horse can look after themselves and he has no stock."

Nicu had years of experience in reading his customer's faces and controlling his own expression. He sensed that the man Renko was not telling the truth and he had noticed the large knife in his belt. He knew that he would have to be very careful in what he said to avoid provoking the man in any way.

"Would you like to have a look at what I have in my van? My prices are good for a fellow Tigani. I can tell that you are one of us."

Making no response, Tigo climbed the steps and looked inside. The large van was fitted with shelves packed with a wide variety of items. Tigo bought food, a waterproof jacket, trousers, shirt and two cartons of 12-bore cartridges with money he had found hidden in the kitchen. Nicu thanked him for the money and for a moment his eyes seemed to be studying Tigo's face. Tigo tensed and Nicu looked at the farm and barn and with a big smile told Tigo it would take him a year at least to make up for the neglect of the buildings.

Just for a moment Tigo thought about killing Nicu, but the man was a Tigani too, just making a living and although it was easy to bury bodies, it would be difficult to hide such a large van. The man seemed to have accepted his story and Tigo would be riding on within a week. After shaking hands again Nicu climbed back into his van and drove slowly away with a black cloud of diesel smoke trailing behind in the morning air. As he left the farmhouse behind, Nico began to relax and wondered why something about the man Renko's face seemed odd to him.

Tigo had worked on the farm buildings and field because he was bored and wanted to restore his strength by keeping himself busy. Now he realised the work had helped to make Nicu accept his explanation for living on the farm. If he mentioned his presence to other customers in the area, there might be some visitors, but Tigo would stay with the same story.

That night he was able to drink coffee again with three spoons of sugar and opened a can of beans and bacon to go with two eggs from the farm chickens. He felt relaxed for the first time since his wild ride through the forest after he was shot. He was a chief and once he was in Dunakeszi he would make himself every bit as important as Renko had been. He guessed that Nico had noticed the paler skin on his face where he had shaved off his beard, but men often removed their beards when they showed too many grey hairs, as his had done.

As he drove the van to the next customer, Nicu remembered seeing a wanted poster for a bearded Tigani with long hair and ringlets. There was a reward of 500,000 Leu and Nicu had thought how the money would allow him to replace his old van. The man Renko had somehow reminded him of the face on the poster, but money was worth nothing if it cost your life and Nicu had kept himself calm and friendly when facing the big Tigani. Three days later he entered a small town and looked again at a wanted poster pinned to a tree. He covered the beard and ringlets with his hands and it made the likeness look very similar to Renko's face. There was a police station in the next town and the next day he reported his suspicions to the sergeant inside.

The sergeant read the report that the wanted man was armed and dangerous, but with one man sick and another needed on the desk, he asked for help in checking if the man seen by Nicu was this Tigo, involved in the shooting near Pasiti. It was a further two days before a team of four armed policemen approached the remote Borel farm and after carefully checking the buildings, entered the house and found it empty. If Tigo had been the man living there, he had now moved on. A full report was sent to Police HQ at Bucharest, which was read by Major Chisca and Lieutenant Bumbesco. The major chided his assistant about their most wanted fugitive.

"So if he was shot at the crossroads how did he manage to avoid our men, ride furiously cross country and then find himself a safe haven near Sibiu. The report says there is no sign of the old man who owned the farm and we can assume his body is buried there. Tigo must be making his way west and that means he is probably headed for Hungary. All we can do now is warn the Hungarian police that we believe our killer Tigo is heading their way."

"I would be willing to help the Hungarians sir, since we want Tigo for murders here."

"If the Hungarians report that Tigo is there and is threatening their people, I will offer your services, since it was your good work that proved his guilt."

After Nicu drove away, Tigo tried on the new clothes and looked in a mirror. He could see that his hairline and chin were still pale where he had clipped his hair and shaved his beard, which must have been what Nicu had seen. Perhaps it was just idle curiosity by Nicu, but his survival instinct had saved him before and it drove him now as he began gathering his few belongings and preparing to continue his journey to Hungary the following morning. He was not yet fully recovered from his wounds, but he would be able to ride slowly towards the border and it was better than staying and risking death, or prison.

The following night, he slept in the forest and ate food which he carried with him. After another three days of steady riding, he reached a Tigani village near Reghin and was given food and shelter for the night. Watching an armed horseman ride into his village, the leader gave him a warm welcome and did not let him out of his sight, or relax until the stranger rode on the next morning. One week later, Tigo reached the outskirts of Dunakeszi after a long and tiring journey. He was saddle sore and tired and hoped that his friend Gunari would be able to find him secluded accommodation where he could rest and fully regain his strength. He also hoped Gunari would be able to find him more ammunition for his rifle, since he had been unable to buy any during his journey.

Riding near the Tigani village at Dunakeszi, he met an old woman driving a horse and cart and asked her if she knew a Tigani named Gunari. She told him that Gunari lived in the big house with the car parked outside, but because he was such a busy man, it was not easy to find him in. Thanking the woman, Tigo rode past the village and rested beside his grazing horse in a copse of trees. He planned to call on Gunari when it was dark to avoid being seen calling on his friend. The Romanian soldier seemed to have done very well for himself and Tigo hoped he would remember the help he had given him during his stay at his village. After Tigo had told him about his stepbrother Renko and his mother's treatment by the Pusztai family, Gunari had sworn he would do all he could to help Tigo pursue his claim to the Pusztai lands.

Once darkness had fallen, Tigo walked back to the village, but kept to the shadows until he reached the house with the car outside. He was surprised that the door was not locked and slowly entered and made his way to a lighted room, but there was no sign of Gunari. Then he was gripped from behind and a knife was held against his throat.

"Who are you and why are you in my house?"

"Gunari, it's me, Tigo. I have ridden from Romania to see you."

Gunari turned him round and studied his face carefully for some time before wrapping his arms around him and leading him into his home.

"Welcome, my friend. You do not look as you were at Budestin. What have you done with your long hair and you have no beard. I thought that you had come to steal from my house."

Tigo was given food and drink as he told his friend about the shooting at Pasiti where he was wounded and the terrible ride through the forest when he just managed to cling to his horse. He failed to mention the old farmer he had killed, but described his long journey across the remote areas of Romania before reaching the border. After choosing an isolated patch of thick forest and using night darkness as cover, he had been able to cross unseen into Hungary so that he could reach Dunakeszi.

Knowing that Tigo was a wanted fugitive, Gunari warned his friend that he must be careful to avoid being seen and could not stay in his house. The news that there was a stranger in the area would be quickly picked up by the local police. The Romanian police would already be working with their contacts in the Hungarian police who would probably visit his home. He agreed to find Tigo somewhere to stay and took him in his car to near where his horse was tethered. Driving slowly, he then led him to a vardo, which he kept in a secluded part of the forest. After giving his friend a supply of food, Gunari promised to get him more ammunition for his rifle.

Tigo should be safe in the vardo for as long as he needed to pursue his claim on the Pusztai lands. Gunari promised he would help as much as he could, but Tigo must not openly involve him in his actions. Gunari was very satisfied with the new life he had built and did not want it put at risk. After years of denigration and patronising treatment because he was a Tigani, he was now respected by both his own people and the local mine officials. He had finally achieved his dream. Although he tried hard, Tigo could not persuade his friend to change his mind and help him to kill Demeter and get his lands.

Left alone in his vardo home, Tigo thought about the times when he and Gunari had planned how they would recover the Pusztai lands after his brother Renko had been cheated out of his inheritance because he was a Tigani. Gunari was very bitter about his own life as a soldier and the way he had been constantly overlooked for promotion because he was Tigani. After being sent to spy on Tigo, he had found a new friend and new purpose in his life. Gunari believed that he was smarter than those who had constantly treated him as a second-class citizen and was determined to prove it. It was while the two friends were hunting in the forest that the soldiers had come to the village, killed Tigo's mother and destroyed it. When they returned and looked around at the burnt-out buildings, the two men vowed they would take revenge on all those responsible.

The long journey had left Tigo totally exhausted and he knew that he would have to rest and build up his strength before beginning to stalk the Pusztai man. After he had watched his brother killed at Budestin, he had found money and documents in his brother's house. He had more than enough for his needs and he knew where Renko had hidden more documents and details of his bank deposits in the Dunakeszi area. During the communist era, when Renko served in the Hungarian Secret Police, he had built up dossiers on many of the present-day government officials. They would not want to have their previous associations and activities with the communists revealed and could be persuaded to help Tigo when he claimed the Pusztai lands.

Renko had also hidden the wedding certificate proving that his mother Bella had married Demeter's grandfather and Renko was also Tigo's older half-brother. Anxious to protect his mother's reputation, Renko had not told Tigo that his mother was suspected of murdering Demeter's grandmother to allow her to seduce her husband. Bella was lucky to escape prison because her vile act could not be proved. The marriage was annulled and Bella and little Renko had been expelled from the estate. Tigo was not a blood relative of the Pusztai family and would have no chance of making a claim, unless Demeter, the last surviving family member was dead. At Budestin, Tigo had told Gunari only about the wedding between his half-brother's mother and Demeter's grandfather to convince him that he had a just claim on the Pusztai lands. He knew that he would have no chance unless he was able to prove that he was the last surviving relative of the Pusztai family. Now that he had reached Dunakeszi he would make sure that he would be that last surviving relative.

Chapter 27
Confrontation

After the Russian Mafia gang was killed in the police rescue of Roseanne Dempsey, Randil Security operation gained new clients when much of the credit for the capture was given to Jack Randil, with subtle comments in the *Liverpool Echo* about the ex-city councillor. His brother-in-law Greg was having difficulty coping with extra customers and Jack persuaded him to take on an assistant to share the burden. Although Jack had only told his wife and squash partner Inspector Peter Kilshaw about his contacts with Gary Dempsey, the demise of the Young Guns gang was also somehow linked to his name. He noticed the special looks he received when attending public functions and meeting with his employees. Patrons of the Devine Fitness Studio quizzed his big friend Joe about Jack's involvement and smiled knowingly when he told them he knew nothing.

Jack had telephoned Demeter every few days to check on his safety and ask if there was any sign of Tigo in the area, but he was told that he should return for the coming Hun-Al Board Meeting and there was no need for an earlier visit. Demeter was at his desk at the refinery when he was visited by the local police and given information from Bucharest that the Romanian police had just missed capturing Tigo. They now believed that he was headed for the Hungarian border on his way to Dunakeszi. With the Board meeting only two weeks away, Demeter decided to say nothing to Jack, but warned his servants to keep a sharp watch for any unknown visitors near the house.

Two days later, Jack received a frantic telephone call from Demeter, who told him that shots were fired at the house and a man had then forced his way inside the kitchen and shot his housekeeper Aranka. Jack booked his flight on the first plane to Budapest and when he arrived, he saw the tall figure of his friend waiting at the customs barrier. With his luggage in the car boot, Demeter then drove off to the Pusztai house and gave Jack a full account of the shooting.

After Theresa's horse was shot when she was out riding with Demeter, security at the house was improved and the old window shutters were replaced. Although he had three hunting rifles, Demeter made sure that he and his gardener Janos could quickly arm themselves from storage cupboards on the ground and first floors. Theresa returned to Durham University and many days passed without incident so that security levels were gradually relaxed. Demeter wanted to make a number of proposals at the coming board meeting and decided he would have fewer interruptions if he stayed at home to complete his preparation. After working most of the day in his study, he had a headache and decided he needed fresh air, so taking a number of trade periodicals to read, he sat out on the terrace.

Aranka had just brought him a coffee, but before he could drink it the heavens opened and rain began to pour down. Demeter ran for shelter through the kitchen door, but was already soaked by the driving rain. Aranka glanced out of the kitchen window and noticing that Demeter had left his magazines on the table, asked him if she should fetch them in. After telling her that he would get them, he was reaching for a waterproof coat when Janos told him he was already soaked and he should stay and dry himself. Janos put on the waterproof coat and ran out into the rain and collected the magazines. As he was hurrying back to the kitchen, he heard two loud shots and the sound of smashing glass. Demeter also heard the gunfire and knew that they must protect themselves.

He collected two revolvers from a cupboard and giving one to Janos told him to check on the dining room windows and make sure the front door was bolted. Having secured the ground floor, he ran upstairs to look for any signs of the attackers outside the house. After looking through the front and back windows he could see sign of any intruders and then he heard a crash and Aranka screaming downstairs. He ran back downstairs to the kitchen and saw a tall man in the kitchen holding a rifle after forcing his way in through the kitchen door. The man was pointing a rifle at Aranka and Demeter immediately raised his gun and fired at him. His bullet was on target, but struck the wooden stock of the rifle and knocked it out of the intruder's hands. Unfortunately, the rifle went off and Aranka cried out and dropped to the floor. As Demeter reacted automatically and dodged behind the door entrance the intruder ran out into the pouring rain. Janos rushed into the kitchen and quickly knelt down to attend to his wife.

Furious with himself for not taking his opportunity to fire again at the man, Demeter ran outside after him. The dusk shadows and pouring rain made it impossible to see more than a few feet and after running around the house, he heard the sounds of a horse galloping away and knew the man had escaped. Demeter rang for an ambulance and then contacted the local police to seek their help. Fortunately, the bullet had only grazed Aranka's shoulder and although she had a painful wound, the bullet had missed her bones. Janos removed her blouse, which was soaked with her blood and was holding a cold compress to her shoulder when they heard the ambulance arrive outside. Two medical orderlies hurried into the kitchen and after packing the wound to stem the blood flow, took her to the ambulance and drove off to the hospital. As they were leaving, a police car arrived and a sergeant and constable hurried into the house and spoke with Demeter.

Two armed policemen searched around the house, but the rain was still heavy and dampened their enthusiasm, as well as making it difficult to look for signs left by the gunman. The sergeant examined the gun and said he would get it checked for fingerprints and return in the morning to make a thorough search. A constable remained to keep guard in case the gunman returned. Jack complimented Demeter on his accurate shot.

"Good shooting Demeter in the heat of the moment and the man was lucky his rifle saved him from a serious wound. Let's hope he is not so lucky when we catch up with him. Do you know whether your bullet went clean through the gun stock?"

"It struck the wooden stock just short of the magazine, or according to the policeman, it could have been diverted into his body. It went right through the wood but must then have hit a metal buckle, or even knife the man was carrying because the bullet was flattened and not quite clear of the wood."

"It must have been his lucky night, but he lost his gun after nearly losing his life as well. Perhaps he will now leave you alone, or he might be so furious that he missed shooting you that he will get another gun and try again. Did the police find anything when they searched outside the house?"

Demeter shook his head.

"I thought they would find the two cartridge cases outside from where he shot at Janos, but the police think he picked them up. They found the cartridge case after he shot Aranka in the kitchen, but any footprints outside would have been washed away by the rain. They are keeping a lookout for any strangers who have moved into the area, but unfortunately they don't have enough men to make a thorough search."

"That worries me, Demeter. The shooter must have searched for the cartridges in heavy rain to take them away with him, then decided to break into your house and attack you. Whoever he is, the man is a determined killer, but he was foolish to take shots at Janos as he was running through heavy rain. Then your sudden appearance in the kitchen must have shocked him into panicking and losing his gun. You could well have wounded him with your shot. We spent two days in Budestin with Tigo, so do you think it could have been him who attacked the house after escaping from Romania?"

"The man was tall and well built, but he had short hair and no beard and his face was thin and sort of blotchy. He was not the Tigo I remember from Budestin."

"The Romanian police think he was coming here after you, but perhaps he had help, or he could have cut off the long hair and ringlets and shaved off the beard to change his appearance when making his escape from Romania. That would leave lighter patches on his face. My guess is that it was Tigo."

They arrived at the Pusztai house and Jack was introduced to Janos, who told him his wife would be coming home in two days and she wanted him to teach her how to shoot. The next time anyone broke into the house she promised she would shoot first. The dining room windows had already been repaired and two men were fitting a new and very substantial kitchen door without the glass panes of the original. The new front door was a solid mahogany design, which would be very hard to force, or break. After their evening meal together, Jack asked Demeter to show him local maps of the area. They marked out possible hiding places within reasonable riding distance for anyone wanting to attack the house. Jack was not a good horseman, but remembered that Demeter had an alternative.

"Do you still have that Kawasaki quad bike you use to scoot around your land?"

Demeter admitted that it was in an old shed at the back of the house, but he had not used it for a while. They went out to check it over and Janos said he would top up the oil and fill the petrol tank. The 750-cc engine and light frame made it ideal for riding over the hills and grasslands.

"If I can borrow one of your rifles and a box of ammunition, I will spend tomorrow looking for our friend before he has time to get himself another gun. If you give me a five-gallon can as well, I should be able to get to most of the places we marked on the map."

If it was Tigo on his own, or with a helper and he was lucky enough to find them, Jack was determined they would either go to prison, or be shot. At breakfast the next morning, Jack had an idea on identifying the attacker.

"Since the rifle was shot out of his hands, the local police should find the attacker's prints on it. Why not ring our friend Herceg at Budapest Police HQ and ask if copies can be sent to that smart Romanian policeman Bumbesco, who is very keen to arrest Tigo for murder? He can then check to find if it was Tigo. If you wait for it to work through the local police it will take weeks and they don't have Tigo's fingerprints to check against. Did the police sergeant tell you what type of rifle was used?"

"Yes, he thought it was a copy of the AK 47 Kalashnikov which had been fitted with a scope for better accuracy. It could have been made here in Hungary, or in China. It's a good idea to contact the Romanians Jack. I will phone Herceg from the office while you are out on your hunting trip on the Kawasaki, but be careful. By the way, it now has a brand-new seat so you won't be able to complain about getting injured this time. Be very careful, you don't know how many you could be facing out there. If you do find them, call the police and let them go in and arrest them."

"Tigo is a Tigani and their village is only about eight miles from here. Did the local police check to see if there were any new arrivals?"

"Yes, it was the first place they checked the day after the shooting, but they found no one and nothing suspicious. They also visited Gunari, who has a house there, but he claims to have had no contact with Tigo."

"That man is very smooth and very helpful, but I have a feeling that the ready smile could cover some deep and nasty feelings. Is he still not speaking, or has he finally learned Hungarian?"

"I have heard him speaking some Hungarian, so either he has learned the language, or he was fooling us when we first met him."

"The man is a manipulator and I suspect he was the brains behind the attacks against your railway and the mine. Can I borrow your binoculars and a phone for tomorrow, just in case I get lost, or your Kawasaki breaks down?"

Chapter 28
Determination

After spending five days resting and walking through the woods to do some hunting with the extra ammunition Gunari had brought him, Tigo could restrain himself no longer and he rode towards the Pusztai house. He followed the directions given to him by Gunari, since although his friend would not involve himself with attacks on the Pusztai man, he was willing to give Tigo all the help he needed to attack the last family member.

After the long rides in the previous weeks, he found the distance no problem, although Gunari had planned a route which used available cover and avoided areas where he might be seen. He had not told Gunari about his attempt to shoot Demeter when he had seen him riding with a companion. When he saw that he had shot the horse of the rider with Demeter, he did not know if the two were armed and rode off. Each day he timed his ride to reach the Pusztai house just before dusk and took care to shield the lenses of the binoculars Gunari had given him to avoid reflecting the dying sun's rays. He had watched the movements of the Tigani man and woman who worked for Demeter and also caught glimpses of Demeter arriving in his car each afternoon and entering the house.

It was a short walk for Demeter from his car to the house and he usually walked quickly. Tigo knew his shooting skills were not good enough to be sure of killing the moving man. If he missed, the police would be looking for him and Demeter would be on his guard. If he waited close to the house he might be seen and Demeter could be armed. After five days of watching and then riding back to the vardo, Tigo was looking through the binoculars at the back of the house and expecting Demeter to arrive home by car. He was surprised to catch a glimpse of his prey sitting at a table on the terrace, when he should have been at work, or returning. Tigo worked his way carefully around the house and then it began to rain very heavily, just as Demeter in a hooded raincoat ran outside to pick some papers up from a table. Seizing his chance, Tigo fired two quick shots at him, but missed and smashed a window. Furious with himself for failing, he still remembered his advice from Gunari to always pick up empty cartridge cases.

Demeter had run back to the house and entered the kitchen. The lights were on, but the curtains were drawn and he could not see inside. Moving closer, he tried the kitchen door and was annoyed to find it locked. Looking at the door with its glass panels he saw it was not very sturdy. Suddenly, his frustration peeked and made him ignore all the training he had received from Gunari to always remain unseen. He kicked the door hard near the lock and it flew open and allowed him to run into the kitchen. A woman was standing near the window and when she saw him, she began screaming. As he raised his rifle to make her keep quiet, she picked up a large kitchen knife and held it pointed towards him. At the same time, Demeter appeared on the far side of the kitchen, with a gun in his hand. For a moment both men glared at each other, then Demeter fired at him and he felt a blow to his stomach and pulled the trigger by accident, since he had not wanted to harm the woman. The impact of the round knocked the rifle from his hands and desperate to avoid being shot again, he ran outside and made for his horse.

In the heavy rain and darkness, he was able to ride away from the house unseen and headed the horse back to the vardo, cursing himself for his rash behaviour and for losing his rifle. As he rode, he could feel every movement bringing waves of pain to his stomach and he dreaded to think how badly he had been injured by Demeter. He began thinking how he would explain his stupid behaviour to Gunari. The man never seemed to show any emotion, but when angered he was always able to keep perfectly calm and harness his cold fury to retaliate. Once he was inside the lighted vardo, he removed his jacket and saw the deep dent in his ornate belt buckle, which had saved him from Demeter's bullet. If it had not been blocked by his buckle, it would certainly have been far more serious than the wounds he had suffered in Romania. A large purple bruise was already forming on his stomach around the tear in his flesh made by the bullet tip. The round must have passed though the wooden stock of the gun, before hitting his buckle. As he soaked the painful wound with a wet cloth, he knew he had been very lucky to escape from the Pusztai house. He thought about giving up his dream of becoming a rich landowner and returning to Romania, but decided it was worth risking his life and there was no future for him in Romania. The man he needed to kill was only eight miles away and older brother Renko had already killed Demeter's sister. He must now kill the brother.

He hoped to persuade Gunari to find him another rifle, or even a revolver, but a handgun would mean having to get close to his victim who would probably be armed. It would be unwise to tell Gunari about his failed attack on the Pusztai kitchen and instead, he would claim a lucky shot from Demeter had struck his gun. At least he had remembered to pick up his empty cartridge cases. He knew that Gunari was away at another village for a few days and he would have to avoid any further visits to the Pusztai house until he had another weapon. After his attack on the house, the police could be guarding it, or Demeter's friend, the man called Jack might return and would come after him. His foolish behaviour and failed attempt on Demeter would now make it much harder to kill the man. Two days later under cover of darkness, Gunari walked in to the vardo and sat down facing Tigo without saying a word. Unable to remain silent as he sensed the cold anger in his friend, he stood up and reached for a can of Dreher beer.

"It's good to see you Gunari. Would you like a beer?"

His friend waved away the proffered drink and glared at him.

"The police searched my house yesterday when I was away and they were back again this afternoon to ask me about you. I told them I met you in Romania, but have not seen you for some time. If they find you, you will tell them the same and you must leave this vardo tomorrow. I bought it from another Tigani and if you were found using it, I would be suspected."

Tigo was shocked to hear that he must give up his refuge and desperately tried to get his friend to help him.

"Is there somewhere I can stay, at least until I become the new owner of the Pusztai lands?"

"After your foolish attempt to kill Demeter the other night, he is in little danger of losing his properties to you. I was told that you also left your rifle behind before you ran out of his house to escape on your horse. Have you forgotten all the advice I gave you about never being seen? Because you are my friend, I will help you, but you must not take away all the goodwill and respect I have built up here in Dunakeszi. I have brought you a tent and food as well as a rifle and ammunition. Put up the tent only at night because they will be looking for you and will see it in daylight. I don't want to know where you are hiding, but will leave food and any messages in the hidden compartment in the vardo. If we need to send messages, we can put them on the bottom of the compartment I leave the food in. Fortunately, the police did not find this rifle when they searched my house. I bought it from a local man and I would be very unhappy if you lost, or damaged it. I have brought that special package you wanted, but it is very dangerous so be careful how you handle it and remember all the instructions I gave you about using it. You will have no chance of taking the land from Demeter unless you follow the training I gave you when we were together in the mountains. You must leave the vardo tomorrow morning and must not sleep here again. Make sure that you clean up any signs that show you were here and do not make any more stupid mistakes."

Without another word Gunari left and Tigo suddenly remembered the story he had planned to tell him to excuse his impetuous behaviour. The police must have told Gunari all about his actions at the Pusztai house. Left alone, he examined the small tent and food, as well as the rifle and the special package. It was a Kalashnikov like the one he had dropped, but better made and fitted with a good quality scope. He was thick skinned enough to quickly forget the criticism of his actions because with this excellent weapon he could kill Demeter from a good distance. After a few weeks had passed he would use Renko's incriminating documents to persuade senior officials to help him with the claim to the Pusztai lands.

With his few belongings, it did not take him long to bundle everything up inside the rolled-up tent. He would be ready to ride off early in the morning and leave no signs that he had ever been in the vardo. He would have to find himself an abandoned house, or hut to give him and his horse extra shelter from the autumn winds, but in spite of his failed attempt, he was still confident that he could take over the Pusztai lands. With his knowledge of the area, Gunari could at least have given him directions to suitable hiding places, but in his angry mood Gunari only wanted him out of the vardo to protect his own safety.

When Gunari was told about the failed attack on Demeter, he realised that he could no longer control, or help Tigo without risking everything he had gained since leaving Budestin. His future could only be protected if Tigo was killed before he could implicate his mentor. Gunari decided that he must take advantage of any opportunities which would allow him to destroy Tigo and protect himself.

Chapter 29
Exploration

It was a clear day with a bite in the air and Jack was glad that he had on a thick coat as the Kawasaki surged away from the house. The powerful machine-made light work of climbing the grassy slopes and Jack planned to work his way through each of the likely sites suggested by Demeter. The two men had decided that he would work to a ten-mile radius around the house, assuming that the attacker would not want to remain too near, but settle for an easy horse ride to keep watch on the Pusztai house. There was plenty of grass for the horse and Jack was guessing that it would be tethered during most of the day, before being ridden out in the late afternoon. The attacker would want to avoid daylight when he might be seen.

Demeter's grandfather had made full use of the land by growing wheat and maize, as well as owning a herd of Longhorn cattle. After the war and during the period of communist control, the land was neglected and the stock was either killed, or stolen. In the new democratic Hungary, farming was gradually expanding and barns and cattle shelters were being repaired, or replaced. Jack was carefully checking buildings and wooded areas on his list after studying them beforehand with the binoculars. He wanted to spot anyone sheltering inside, before they saw him. His army experience with the paratroops was once again proving useful. At midday he was riding near a ruined stone shell with most of the roof missing and a group of twenty or so cattle grazing nearby. His sensitive nose picked up the aroma of coffee and wood smoke, which warned him that the building was occupied. He drove to the side of the building and switched off the engine of the Kawasaki.

The noise would have alerted anyone inside to his presence, but if they were hostile, they would be watching the only entrance. He edged up to a window opening and carefully looked inside. He saw an old horse eating hay from a trough built into the stone wall. Then he looked at a figure sitting in front of a small fire and facing a pot hung from an iron trivet. When the man saw Jack at the window with a rifle trained on him his face showed his fright. Leaping to his feet the man raised both hands above his head and began pleading with Jack in a foreign language. Raising his hand and lowering the rifle, Jack tried to reassure the man that he meant him no harm and walked around to join him near his fire.

When Jack was appointed to the Hun-Al Board he began learning Hungarian and he guessed that the man was a Tigani speaking his own language. Many Tigani also spoke Hungarian and by using his limited vocabulary and sign language, Jack was able to communicate with the man. His name was Robi and he was collecting cattle, which had been allowed to follow the lush grass during the summer, so that they could be put in fenced areas as winter approached and fodder had to be provided.

After explaining that he was looking for a renegade horseman who had shot the housekeeper at the Pusztai house, the man immediately wanted to help. He knew Aranka and respected Demeter as a good friend of the Tigani. Robi spent days and nights rounding up the cattle and he had seen a lone rider in the distance on two occasions. Taking Jack outside the building he showed the direction the man came from and where he had headed. Jack had brought food for his lunch, which he shared with Robi, who in turn provided him with very strong black coffee. Thanking the man for the coffee and his help, Jack drove off in the direction the rider had come from.

After half an hour he reached the edge of the forest, which was too thick to allow him to use the quad bike. Since it was a remote area, he disabled the machine and taking his gun he began walking along the tree line to look for any trails, or tracks made by a horse. After walking south for an hour, he came to a dirt track entering the forest and when he checked the surface there were tyre tracks. Since it was late afternoon and it would take him an hour to walk back to the quad bike, he decided to postpone following the track until the next day.

After the evening meal, he told Demeter about his meeting with Robi and the dirt track leading into the forest. His friend tried to persuade Jack to call in the police, but Jack was adamant that this was something he wanted to do quickly and in his own way. Demeter had surprising news from Budapest Police HQ,

"That Romanian policeman Bumbesco is determined to get Tigo and arranged to have the prints checked as a top priority. The prints on the gun we found are positively Tigo's. Your guess about him cutting his hair and shaving off his beard was right. I got a good look at him in the kitchen, but didn't recognise him. Now Bumbesco is trying to convince our Colonel Herceg that he should be allowed to join us in the hunt, but after hearing what Tigo did to two Romanians, I don't think he wants to bother with extradition."

"Bumbesco is a terrier and very smart. He would be a good man to have with us and as a double murderer Tigo should be sent back to Romania, dead or alive."

"I agree with you Jack. Bumbesco would make an ideal companion in your search. I will telephone Herceg tomorrow morning and do my best to persuade him that you need the extra help, which would save Hungarian expense."

Early the next morning Jack drove off and headed straight for the dirt road leading into the forest. Within minutes he was startled to see a large wooden caravan parked in a small clearing. After slamming on the brakes, he gripped his rifle and jumped down to the ground, using the Kawasaki as cover as he studied the caravan for signs of life. After looking carefully through the binoculars, he was beginning to think the house on wheels was empty, when he heard the sound of a car engine approaching. He watched as an old Dacia saloon drove up and a man got out and stood looking at Jack as he crouched behind his machine, with a rifle cradled in his arms.

"Is that you Mr Randil?"

Jack recognised Gunari and was able to understand him although he spoke in halting Hungarian, which was a big improvement on his complete silence during their first meetings. Jack stood up and walked towards him, with his rifle held trail style in his left hand and the Romanian greeted him.

"Are you on a hunting drive in these woods Mr Randil?"

"Hello Gunari. I am actually hunting for the man who shot Demeter's housekeeper and appears to have ridden this way on his horse when he escaped."

"Oh yes. The police told me about the attack. I do not understand why anyone would want to attack Demeter, who has always been a very good friend to the Tigani people."

"We now know that the man who shot Aranka was Tigo, the half-brother of Renko, who was a long-time enemy of the Pusztai family."

"I know Tigo and when we met at his village in Romania, he was a good host and we spent time together hunting in the forest. He told me about the tragic death of his brother and some details of the dispute between Renko and the Pusztai's. As a fellow Tigani, I convinced him that he must learn to read and write and he began taking lessons. While I was with him, I never heard him make any threats against Demeter, but perhaps something happened after I left. Did you think Tigo was living in my vardo?"

"It would certainly be an ideal place for him to hide and it is an easy ride to the Pusztai house."

"I would be very angry if he has been hiding in my vardo. When I bought it, I had to spend many hours making repairs and it is my treasure and somewhere for me to come to relax. Would you like to look inside?"

Jack nodded his head and followed as Gunari led the way and climbed up the wooden entry steps. The interior was beautifully fitted out and showed the amount of time and effort lavished on it by Gunari. Everything was very neat and tidy and certainly showed no signs of being used as a refuge. As he stood beside Gunari, Jack's keen sense of smell told him something very relevant to his search, but he said nothing and instead complimented Gunari on his 'treasure'. They left the vardo and Jack said he was going to drive on and continue his search. Before leaving he had one question.

"You have done well to run your own car and I congratulate you on settling in so well here. You must find driving more comfortable than riding. Do you keep a horse as well?"

Shaking his head, Gunari replied that he had never been much of a rider and was much happier with his car. As Jack rode away, his mind was turning over the possibilities on why Gunari had lied about someone, probably Tigo, having stayed in his vardo. Jack was very familiar with the distinctive odour of horses and obviously as Tigo spent time on a horse, his clothes absorbed the smell, which was still present in the vardo.

After watching the big man walk away and as he was returning to the vardo, Gunari thought about the Englishman and wondered how he had been able to trace Tigo to the isolated forest area so quickly. Fortunately, the inside was immaculate and he was fairly sure that he had convinced Jack that no one had been staying there. Somehow though he still sensed that the man had his suspicions and he knew that if that was the case, Jack would keep prying. He had spent too much time and energy building his privileged position in the area to have it all put at risk by a nosey foreigner. The man would have to be stopped and he decided he would ask Tigo to repay him for helping with food and the replacement gun by killing Jack. He wrote a message on the bottom of the hidden compartment where he was leaving food for Tigo.

Jack spent the rest of the day searching the forest surrounding the vardo in the hope that Tigo would stay in an area which had become familiar to him. If he had left the vardo for some reason, he would still have to find alternative overnight shelter for himself and his horse. Jack tried to divide his search into manageable areas by parking the Kawasaki in different spots and searching the forest alongside. By late afternoon, he had found no signs of Tigo, or his horse and drove back to the Pusztai house. Demeter had not returned, but with her arm and shoulder bandaged, Aranka was supervising as Janos was preparing the evening meal, which was served as soon as Demeter arrived. Jack was reading in the lounge when he heard voices and looked up to see Demeter and was introduced to a smiling Petru Bumbesco, who had joined them from Romania.

The two men shook hands and all three were then hurried to the dining table by an anxious Janos, who was under strict instructions that the meal must be served before it spoiled.

Over their meal together, Jack heard how with the close co-operation of the Hungarian and Romanian police, it had been agreed that Petru should take some holiday and visit Hungary. He had brought with him copies of the file on Tigo's crimes and would be happy to join Jack on a hunting trip in the area. Demeter would provide him with a rifle and if they were attacked by Tigo, they would certainly be within the law to respond in self-defence. Jack updated Petru on his searches and his meeting with Gunari. Since their native tongues were different, the three men conversed in French, which was their only common language.

"You may not know that Gunari was in the Romanian militia Jack and he met Tigo at Budestin when he was sent to investigate the crucifixion of the half-brother Renko. He did not report back as he was ordered and is liable to arrest in my country for failing in his duty and desertion."

Jack nodded his head and Petru continued.

"When the Budestin people attacked our soldiers and killed one, Gunari and Tigo were away somewhere. We discovered that the two men had become close friends and spent much time together. After Budestin was burned down we do not know where the two went, but because Tigo's mother was killed by the soldiers, we think he took his revenge on Commissar Dalca and sergeant-major Dinescu, who was in charge of the soldiers at Budestin."

When Petru described how the two Romanians had been killed, both Jack and Demeter were horrified and could understand why the Romanians were so determined to capture Tigo. Jack had seen enough violence in his clashes with the Liverpool gangs, but the way in which the Romanians had been killed still shocked him.

"Revenge is always a bad thing, but that is barbaric behaviour, even for a thug like Tigo. It was only by luck that his shot did not kill Aranka when he broke in to the kitchen and he was lucky that Demeter's shot hit his rifle. We must stop him and make him pay for his crimes. If Demeter's shot had been only a couple of inches higher, he could be in prison now or dead, but he was probably wounded."

"I have been tracking him for months Jack and wounded him myself in a shootout in Romania. I will help all I can to protect Demeter and catch my renegade countryman."

The next morning, with Jack driving and Petru sharing the seat, the two men headed for the forest where Gunari's vardo was parked. As they were passing the stone barn, Jack saw that the small herd of cattle had gone and stopped near the primitive doorway. It would be an ideal haven for Tigo and both men carried their cocked rifles in front of them as they looked inside.

The sheltered inside of the barn was quite empty. Jack smoothed his hand over the blackened ashes of the fire, but they were cold and Robi must have left very early to move the herd. There was still some hay in the horse trough, but no other signs that Robi had been using it as shelter.

They climbed back on the Kawasaki and continued on to the forest. Since he still had his suspicions, Jack drove along the dirt track and parked alongside Gunari's vardo. There was just a chance that Tigo had returned. Again, the door was not locked and when he looked at the inside, Petru was impressed by the amount of work Gunari had done. Gunari might well be upset about the two trespassing, but they would just have to assure him that they were checking that Tigo was not hiding in the wooden caravan.

Although Petru's sense of smell was not as sharp as Jack's, he too was able to detect a faint trace of horse odour. The layout was very similar to the vardo used by the big Tigani policeman Rudi in the search for Tigo in Romania. Remembering a hidden compartment, which Rudi had shown him, Petru tried sliding part of the panelling at the rear and exposed a small compartment. Peering inside he saw a cardboard box filled with food. There were cupboards over the cooking area and he could not understand why Gunari had chosen the hideaway to store the food.

"Why would Gunari hide food in here Jack? He has left the door unlocked, which shows he is not worried about intruders."

"According to Demeter, the man is very well respected here and is seen as a sort of spokesman for a number of Tigani villages. The locals would know the vardo was his and would not touch it, so you are right Petru, why would he hide food, unless it was intended for someone he would not want to be seen helping."

"I am sure Jack that if we watch the vardo, Tigo will eventually come for his food and we should be able to catch him. He will probably come at night under cover of darkness. Both of them are Romanians and good friends from the reports I read, so it is not surprising that Gunari would be willing to help Tigo, even though he has become a fugitive."

The two men climbed back on the Kawasaki for their return journey to the Pusztai house. In the late afternoon they returned and parked under cover of some trees a mile away. They then walked back to the vardo and settled down in the bushes surrounding the clearing to keep watch for Tigo. Both men were wearing thick outer clothing to protect themselves during their cold night watch. Jack expected him to come on his horse so that he could make a rapid retreat. Petru thought he would come instead on foot to make less noise. They faced a long cold night as they waited to trap the man and discover who was right. Both men were wrong.

Chapter 30
Delusion

After Gunari had left the vardo and Tigo had gathered his belongings for an early morning start, he sat down on the bunk bed to think about what he should do next. He and Gunari had been friends since they first met, but now the man was only interested in himself and would probably not hesitate to betray him to protect his own interests. Knowing that he must now be on the wanted list of the local police, there was a risk in returning to the vardo to collect the food he had been promised.

At the Pusztai house, he could have shot Demeter and since no one knew he was in the area, he could then have 'arrived' and made his claim on the lands. Because he had missed his chance and got carried away by his emotions and blundered into the kitchen, the police would now suspect him if Demeter was killed. He must somehow arrange for Demeter to have an accident instead so that he would not be blamed.

He remembered Renko telling him that his mother Bella had married a local Tigani and had more children when she moved back to the Dunakeszi village. Looking through the small bundle of papers which fortunately had been in his saddlebag, he found the name Pista Botos, who was Bella's husband. They would certainly have a claim on Pusztai lands, since after the divorce, Demeter's grandfather had never remarried. He wondered if he could somehow turn this knowledge to his advantage.

Renko had told him that Bella had died, but Pista could still be alive, or if he had died, perhaps the children would still be alive. If he visited the village when it was dark, he was sure someone would tell him where the Botos family lived. If the Botos helped him to get the Pusztai lands, he could give them money, or they could share the land.

After leaving the vardo, he had suddenly felt the chill in the air with the approach of winter and was sure that snow would soon come. He remembered seeing an old stone building as he rode to the Pusztai house. It was unwise to ride there in daylight, but if he failed to persuade the Botos family to help him, it could be a useful shelter for overnight stays in his tent. Riding through the forest he soon found a stream and good grass to keep his horse fed and watered. Wrapping the tent around himself as a windbreak and propping up some fir branches as cover, he settled down near the tethered horse to wait out the daylight hours. Most of the older Tigani still spoke their own language, but the younger ones spoke mainly Hungarian. At the village he would wait until he could speak with an older Tigani who should be able to understand him.

Time passed slowly and the ground beneath was hard and uncomfortable. Shivering with the cold, he could not stop remembering his comfortable days as leader of his people at Budestin. After his brother Renko came to escape from the Hungarian and French police, everything seemed to fall apart. Everyone wanted to kill Renko and the local women hated him and were eager to strip and torture him in revenge. As leader he should have refused him refuge, but he was family and he offered good money to be allowed to return to his mother's birthplace. Now his only chance of a comfortable new life depended on killing the last Pusztai. In spite of the cold, he fell asleep and when he woke up it was late afternoon and growing dark and time to move.

Saddling his horse, he rode towards the stone barn to find out if it could be a night shelter. After watching the old building carefully first, he crept closer and with his rifle held ahead of him, looked around the inside. Seeing the ashes and hay in the feeding trough he knew it had been used by others for shelter, but was now empty. Leading the horse to the trough, he collected a pile of hay to spread on the ground and settled down near the doorway to watch for visitors as he waited for darkness before riding on.

After waiting until it grew dark, he rode away from the barn towards the Tigani village. As he reached the scattered homes, he led his horse and walked casually along between the semi-derelict wooden houses. After thinking that the people would be suspicious of a stranger, he would say that he was delivering a horse that the Botos family had bought. A villager walked towards him and looked closely at him for a moment. Tigo lifted the reins of the horse and muttered, "Botos." The man pointed to a house at the far end of the road and continued on his way. Excited that he had traced the Botos family without creating suspicion, or having to say a word, Tigo led the horse to the front of the house. He tied the reins to a rickety wooden fence, walked up to the door and knocked. An old man came to the door and stared at the stranger facing him. Tigo accepted that once again luck was with him since Pista Botos was still alive. He would certainly remember Renko and his determination to claim the Pusztai lands.

"I have come a long way to see you Pista. I am Renko's brother Tigo and I want to make you rich."

Pista's face showed apprehension as soon as he heard the name of the secret police chief who had terrorised his people. With Pista standing unmoving, or speaking in the open doorway, Tigo took advantage by pushing past and closing the door. Taking the old man's arm and drawing him into the house he motioned him towards a chair. Tigo sat down opposite and began to explain that Demeter was the last of the Pusztai family and if he died, the land and properties should be passed to Bella's family. Pista and his children would be amongst the richest Tigani's in the country. Pista listened in silence, but finally responded to the big man who spoke his native language with a strange accent.

"I have known the Pusztai children since they were born and Demeter and Arianne have always been good friends to us Tigani. How can we now take their lands from them?"

"My brother Renko killed Arianne and I am willing to kill Demeter so that we can all share in the lands. Why should one man have so much, when we have so little?"

The two argued for some time before Pista agreed to give Tigo and his horse shelter for the night, but insisted that they must wait until his son Panna returned before any further discussion on what Tigo planned. His son would decide whether to help, or turn him away, since Panna's life was still before him, whilst Pista knew his days were already limited. Panna worked at the Hun-Al refinery and spent most evenings with his friends at a local bar. A large part of his working day was taken up clearing out ore, which worked its way under the conveyor belt rollers taking it to the crushers. If it was not regularly cleared out it could build up and jam the rollers moving the belts. It was hard, dusty work, which gave Panna a fierce thirst and led to his frequent visits to local bars. He also enjoyed drinking beer.

Sitting in a chair facing Pista, the warmth inside the house after his busy day outdoors combined to send Tigo off to sleep. He was awakened by the sound of voices as Pista explained the stranger's presence to his son and that he hoped to take possession of the Pusztai lands. Opening his eyes, Tigo looked at the stocky young man standing near his father and was encouraged to see an excited expression showing on Panna's face. Tigo rose to his feet and as the young man began speaking his father translated from Hungarian to the Tigani dialect.

"My son does not understand how you hope to kill Demeter and then claim his lands. He thinks the police will shoot you, or put you in prison before you can claim the lands. The government will then take them over."

"Tell him that with his help, Demeter will die in an accident when we are away and the police will have nothing against us. We can then return and make a family claim on the Pusztai lands."

With the father making the translation, Tigo then explained in detail what he had in mind and the part he wanted Panna to play. When the son heard the full translation, he beamed at Tigo and then threw his arms around the shoulders of the bigger man. He was willing to help Tigo, who was welcome to take shelter in their home. After years of persecution and deaths, the Pusztai lands were now only days away from yet another attack from the Tigani relatives of Renko's mother Bella. Tigo could tell that snow would soon come and then he and Panna would begin their work to bring about the accident to kill Demeter. Meantime the two would keep a close watch on Demeter's movements and in particular his route from the refinery to his house. Snow was the forecast and when it came, they would act.

Gunari soon learned about the stranger leading a horse who wanted to find the Botos house. He had a close relationship with all the villagers and encouraged them to tell him about any unusual happenings, or visitors. He guessed that Tigo had disregarded his warnings and now hoped to involve the Botos family in his plan to kill Demeter. At first, he was consumed with anger that by his stupidity the fool was putting his hard-won position in the Tigani community at risk. Quickly getting his emotions under control, he directed his energy instead to considering the best way to rid himself of the man who now posed such a dangerous threat. He would wait and watch, but make sure that he was aware of all Tigo's plans by having Pista Botos keep him fully informed. He would then choose the moment to remove the threat and secure his future.

After spending a seemingly endless night watching for Tigo near the vardo, Jack and Petru were stiff and very cold as they made their way back to the Kawasaki for the return drive to the Pusztai house. As a hunting man, Petru was accustomed to spending hours waiting for prey, which often eluded him. Jack was not as patient and was frustrated that Tigo was able to shelter and move around the area at will. He was sure that the Romanian must be receiving help, or perhaps had an accomplice. When he was speaking to Gunari inside the vardo, he sensed that the man was not telling them everything he knew about Tigo. Surely, the man would not want to jeopardise his comfortable lifestyle by sheltering a wanted fugitive.

When Demeter arrived back from his work at the refinery, the three men agreed that it was pointless to spend more time watching the vardo. Either Tigo had decided to return to Romania, or he had found local help and shelter. They would just have to remain on their guard and wait until Tigo made his next move. Petru was on special detachment from his usual work, but because of the nature of Tigo's crimes in Romania he assured Demeter that he could arrange a limited extension to trap Tigo. Jack was turning over the possible reasons for Tigo trying to kill Demeter.

"We know that Tigo is a half-brother to Renko, but unlike Renko, he is not a blood relative through the woman Bella, who married your grandfather. He thinks that by killing you, there will be no other relatives to claim the Pusztai estate. He cannot know about Arianne's son Paul, but there may also be family from Bella's second partner. Perhaps, you should tell your colleagues at the mine about Paul and the news will quickly be passed around that he owns half the estate and until you marry Theresa, is also your heir."

Nodding his head, Bumbesco said that this might persuade Tigo to give up and return to Romania. He asked if Bella had any relatives in Dunakeszi and Demeter told him about the Botos family.

"Tigo got hold of his brother Renko's papers and must know about the Botos family. Although they are not blood relatives, they might have a claim if there were no surviving blood relatives. I agree that the Hun-Al Board should be told about Paul, who took his mother's maiden name after his parents were killed in France. The news will soon spread and if we are lucky, it could be enough to send Tigo back to Romania."

Chapter 31
Treachery

Pista Botos gave Gunari full details of Tigo's plan to kill Demeter and then submit a family claim on the Pusztai estates. Renko had explained to his brother how close he had come to killing Demeter by having a heavy lorry force Demeter's car off the road and plunge into the Danube. When snow had built up on the hillside above the road, Tigo and Panna would set explosive charges on the hilltop and detonate them as Demeter was driving below on his way home from the refinery. Avalanches were common during the winter and the accident would appear natural. As Gunari stood at his door and watched old Pista slowly return to his home, snowflakes began to fall.

At the Hun-Al Board meeting Demeter told his colleagues about his nephew and heir Paul Pusztai. The news was well received, especially when it was explained that Paul would be making regular visits to Hungary from his teens to learn the language and become familiar with the business and the country. The secretary taking the notes was a well-known gossip and Demeter was sure the news would spread quickly. After the meeting, Jack borrowed Demeter's car so that he and Petru could drive to the forest area and take a second look at the vardo belonging to Gunari. The temperature had dropped and it was too cold to use the quad bike. Demeter told them he would be able to have a lift home with an employee.

Jack parked at the roadside and the two trudged through the snow to reach the vardo in the woods. The ground and branches were laden with snow, which cascaded down on them as they forced their way through the trees. During their previous visit Petru had opened the secret panel and found the food, but had failed to make a close examination of the interior, which he had regretted afterwards. The snow was now four inches deep and both men were glad to have changed to heavy boots for the visit. Petru wanted to learn something about English weather.

"Do you have snow in your country Jack?"

"Only very little and at times it can even be deeper than this, but it rarely lasts. The problem is that because it so rarely happens, when we do have a heavy fall we get caught out and our farmers have to help in clearing our side roads."

After stamping the snow from their boots, the pair stepped inside the vardo and Petru knelt to take a good look inside the hidden cavity. There was now no food in the box, which was quite empty. They assumed that Gunari had returned and taken it, but there was also a possibility that it had been collected by Tigo. He was about to slide the panel cover back, when a slip of paper fell from the bottom. There was a message on the paper in a language Petru could not read and they decided they would ask someone who spoke the Roma language to translate for them. They agreed that although it had been found in Gunari's vardo, it would not be mentioned, or shown to Gunari. When they got back to the Pusztai mansion they were surprised to find that Demeter had not yet returned from the refinery and there was no message to explain his absence.

Within hours of the board meeting at the refinery, Gunari was told about the young heir Paul Pusztai. He could hardly control his joy when he thought about the effect it would have on Tigo's plans. It was snowing again and adding to the layer from the previous night's fall. Knowing the best spot to plant explosives on the hillside above the river road, he guessed that conditions would be ideal for sending a wave of snow down the steep slope.

Demeter was relieved to hear that a mechanic had finally managed to repair the fault in the car and he would now be able to get his lift home. The car had a heater, but even with his heavy overcoat, he still felt cold as the car pushed its way along the snow-clad road.

Tigo and Panna waited on the hillside after placing two explosive charges near a deep bank of snow and kept watching for Demeter's car to approach along the narrow bend on the road below. Gunari had suggested two charges to create a wide avalanche, which would sweep the car off the road and down to the Danube below. The cold and bitter winds on the exposed

183

hillside soon had both men shivering despite their thick outer clothing. Time passed and with snow blowing in their faces it made it difficult to see anything but the headlights of cars passing below. An hour after the time when Demeter usually passed the spot, with Panna complaining constantly that he was getting frostbite, Tigo had to call off the attempt and they retrieved the explosives to go home. As they were collecting the second package, a car passed below. Tigo clenched his fist and swore after spending almost two hours on the windswept hillside, only to see their target pass safely below as they were leaving.

Jack was first to hear the distinctive note of the diesel car engine and was at the door as a snow-covered figure rushed inside the house thrashing its arms and stamping feet to restore circulation. After sharing large brandies with his friends, Demeter looked at the note found in Gunari's vardo. He was unable to translate the full contents, but did find one word, which he understood to refer to an outsider, or intruder. Unfortunately, the housekeeper and her husband could not read. The only solution was to show the note to a Tigani worker at the refinery the next day, but without explaining where it was found.

Gunari watched from his window as Tigo and Panna returned home and judged from their gloomy faces that their attempt on the hillside had not been a success. He guessed that having failed in their first attempt, they would try again tomorrow and with a heavier fall of snow conditions would be ideal. He could walk in and tell Tigo about the second Pusztai heir, but he now had his own plan, which would be far more satisfying than simply shattering the hopes of the two men. He would have to be sure that he was at the correct spot on the hillside whilst the two Tigani men were waiting for Demeter's car to pass below them on the riverside road.

A new ore-crushing machine was to be switched on at the refinery and rather than remain indoors at the Pusztai mansion, Jack and Petru joined Demeter at the plant to view the monster machine and enjoy the celebratory meal which followed. The roads already had a thick covering of snow, which had fallen during the previous night, but the Mitsubishi with four-wheel drive coped very well. Output from the mine had increased and with the rail link, the volume of ore arriving at the refinery required an expansion in its processing capacity. Demeter was awarded the honour of pressing the starting switch and the watching crowd applauded as there was a throaty roar and the giant machine began crunching up the raw bauxite ore fed into it. Speeches followed and Jack managed to make a small contribution with his limited Hungarian vocabulary.

A wide selection of local food and wine was on display and as Demeter was to be their driver, Petru and Jack were free to enjoy the sweet red Tokaji wine being served. When snowflakes began to fall, the three men decided it was time to make the drive back to the mansion before the river road became impassable. After thanking the staff, they trudged through the yard and hurried into the big Mitsubishi and switched on its heater. The snow level was growing and they needed the dipped headlights full on to have a good view of the road surface ahead. As they approached the stretch running alongside the river, Jack suddenly had a strong premonition of danger and warned Demeter to drive slowly and keep to the hillside of the road, well away from the river edge. When they began driving down the hill where the road was closest to the river, they heard an explosion, quickly followed by a second. Demeter carefully applied the car brakes and managed to steer the skidding car to safety. Looking up they watched as a torrent of snow swept down the hillside and began spilling across the road around them.

Chapter 32
Revelation

Gunari was wearing his warmest clothes, but even after covering himself with a small canvas sheet for protection whilst waiting for Tigo to arrive, the biting cold and chilling wind still seemed to cut right through him. He had never liked horses and normally used his car to travel and show that he was a person of standing. Tonight, he had been forced to borrow a horse and it seemed to know that its rider was inexperienced and no animal lover. It shied away when he took the reins and required constant use of the spurs to move it in the right direction. Anxious to avoid being stranded, he made sure that the animal was very securely hobbled in a sheltered spot to be ready for his return.

Finally, he heard voices and watched as two figures arrived on horseback and made their way on foot to their chosen position below him. After they had laid the two sets of explosives, each waited alongside their respective positions to be ready to light the fuses. Panna was crouched where he would be first to recognise Demeter's familiar car and would signal Tigo. Both men would then light their fuses and climb up the hill to take cover. As the two men concentrated their attention on the road below. Gunari climbed carefully down from the hilltop and laid his own charges above them. His work done, he was glad to return to his primitive shelter and watch the Tigani men and his horse.

Gunari was waiting for the first explosion before pressing the button on his battery-operated detonator. His hands were so numb that he knew he would not have been able to cope with lighting a fuse. Although he had shown Tigo how to use explosives, he had craftily explained only how to operate them with the old-fashioned burning fuse method. His natural instinct had always been to ensure that he kept the best material and skills

186

to himself. Suddenly two explosions sent a wall of snow rolling down the hillside, growing bigger as it poured across the road. Then Gunari's two explosions followed and another wave of snow hurtled down and carried away the two men sheltering below him. Satisfied that his work was done, Gunari wasted no time in rolling up his tarpaulin and scampering back to the horse he had left tethered amongst the trees on the hilltop. The warmth from the horse beneath gradually helped to bring back circulation in his legs as he rode towards the safety and comfort of his home.

A giant wall of snow had swept over the car buried beneath as the bulk of the avalanche surged past and over it before tumbling into the River Danube below. Fortunately, Demeter had managed to steer the car well into the hillside edge of the road and their lives were saved. By driving slowly over the snow-covered road, they had been at the extreme edge of the avalanche aimed at them, since Tigo had timed the explosions on the car's normal speed to have maximum effect. Before they could attempt to climb out through the car windows, there were more explosions and yet another wave of snow poured over the car roof and trapped them inside the Mitsubishi. Relieved that they had survived a deliberate attempt on their lives, they accepted that they would have to wait until help arrived to dig them out. They could not risk using the car heater by switching on the engine because of the danger of being poisoned by the exhaust fumes trapped under the snow cover. Instead, they shared out their clothing to fight off the freezing cold. Demeter used his phone to call the refinery office, explain what had happened and organise a rescue group. He also produced two bottles of Tokaji wine he was taking home.

An hour later, a team of workers arrived and one side of the car was quickly cleared to allow the three men to escape. They were quickly wrapped in warm blankets and given hot drinks. Not only had the wine warmed them, it had also left them less apprehensive about their entombment. The work to clear the road continued and the crushed and lifeless body of Panna was discovered. Now, the perpetrators of the avalanche could be guessed, since Demeter recognised the Botos man and knew that he must have been helping Tigo. A second body was then found and although badly injured, this man was still alive. He was carried to an ambulance and transferred to the local hospital. Demeter followed with his two companions.

The sole survivor had been treated and was badly bruised and bandaged, but despite his changed hairstyle, they immediately recognised Tigo. The doctors told them that with such serious injuries, he would certainly never walk again. Petru was first to speak to the man he had spent so many months pursuing.

"Why did you kill Commissar Dalca and Sergeant Major Dinescu in Romania?"

With a startled expression on his face, Tigo muttered that he did not know who these men were and had nothing to do with their deaths. As Petru explained what had been done to his countrymen, Tigo's face showed that he had guessed who had been responsible for the killings. He had also guessed who was responsible for setting off the explosives intended to kill him and Panna. He told them that when Gunari arrived at his village, they immediately took to each other and went hunting in the forest. Gunari showed him how to shoot, track animals and make his way without leaving signs for others to follow. He also showed Tigo how to use explosives, which they had found in a second world war abandoned German camp. When they returned and found Budestin village burned to the ground by soldiers, Gunari went berserk and told him how he hated the army for despising him as a Tigani. He swore he would get his revenge, but when they parted, Tigo thought his friend had moved to Hungary and he had never mentioned killing any commissar or soldier. He explained how he and Panna were swept down the hillside by explosives placed above them, which must have been set off by Gunari, who wanted them blamed and silenced.

Jack produced the note found in the vardo and shrugging his shoulders, Tigo explained that it was just urging him to kill the foreigner, that is, Jack. Gunari saw Jack as a real threat and wanted him out of the way to protect his position in Dunakeszi. All three were stunned to learn that the quietly spoken advisor to the local Tigani communities was a ruthless killer as well as certainly being responsible for setting the explosive charges at the mine and refinery. In his loyalty to his people, he had also persuaded them to leave their village so that they could not be punished and had succeeded in diverting the rail line.

Jack and Petru persuaded the mine security team to take them back to the Pusztai mansion to collect their rifles before going to Gunari's house. The local police were happy to cooperate with the large local employer and avoid risking their own men. Jack insisted that Demeter remain behind and allow trained hunters to capture Gunari, who would surely hear about the survivor of the avalanche and expect them to come for him. Demeter was not happy about being left out of the chase, but Jack reminded him that Tigo was unlikely ever to trouble him again and Gunari had murdered two Romanian officials and was top of their police wanted list.

After riding back to his house through the snow, Gunari was stiff with the cold, but triumphant for having got rid of the fool Tigo. The bad-tempered horse was less troublesome when it sensed it was on its way back to the comfort of its stable. He had been told by his contacts at the refinery that the foreigner Jack and the Romanian policeman would also be in the car with Demeter. Tonight, he had eliminated all those who threatened his new life in Dunakeszi and the new leader of the mining company would certainly need his help. There was a knock at his door and old Botos wanted to talk to him. After taking him into his house, he was stunned to hear that Panna was dead, but Tigo had survived and been taken to hospital. He knew that his secrets would all be revealed, as Tigo would guess who had set off explosives above them. Sending Botos back to his home, he moved quickly to load his prize possessions into his car, together with a rifle and ammunition. He would drive as far as he could towards the border and then travel on foot to cross into Romania and hide out in one of the Tigani villages. If he was stopped, he was prepared to shoot his way through, or die in the process. He knew that in spite of all his work and planning his new life in Dunakeszi was now finished and did not want to spend the rest of his years in prison, if he was not executed.

As he drove out of the village, he noticed two of the mine security cars driving towards his house. When he saw the cars stop and then turn around and begin to follow him, he accelerated to try to get as far ahead of them as possible. The only route was along the river road, which he knew had now been cleared of the avalanche snow. The following security cars were catching up and he had to drive faster to hold his lead. He was not a good driver and the roads were slippery, which forced him to grip hard on the steering wheel to hold the car in the middle of the road. When he reached the river road, he could see in his mirror that the security cars were close behind. Turning into the sharp bend where Demeter's car had been buried, he realised that he was going too fast. Instinctively, he stamped on the brake pedal, which immediately caused the car to begin skidding sideways across the road. Horrified he watched as it crashed through the roadside fence and plunged down into the River Danube below. Suddenly, there was black water all around him and then it began filling the car. Frantically he tried to force open the car door, but the weight of water was too great and it was immovable. The icy cold water rose slowly up his body and to find air to breath he had to stretch almost to the car roof, but then the car was filled with water and he could breathe no more.

Jumping out of the security cars, Jack and Petru walked to the smashed fence and looked down towards the river below, but could see only blackness. Petru stamped his foot in frustration and turned to Jack.

"Damn, I wanted to take that man back to my country to be tried and executed for his crimes, but drowning in the icy Danube waters is I suppose a fitting end. It will also avoid raising our unfair treatment of the Tigani people, which must have driven him to become a murderer. When he and Tigo returned to find Budestin had been destroyed by soldiers, his years of frustration must have boiled over and he took his revenge on those he considered responsible. Dalca had a bad reputation from his time serving the communist regime, but Dinescu was just doing his duty and following orders.

Tigo must have killed the farmer Butaco and buried the body and although his was not the hand which slit his brother's throat, by allowing it to happen, he caused the deaths which followed. Even after being shot twice, he still managed to escape and made it to Dunakeszi much sooner than we expected.

It was fortunate that he was a poor shot, but nearly killed your lady Theresa and also shot Aranka. He will never ride, or walk again, but will he spend the rest of his life in a Romanian prison, or here in Hungary? My hope is that Hungary will return him to his own country. We are indebted to you Jack for your help in finding the real killer of our citizens."

190

Putting his arm around the shoulders of the Romanian policeman, Jack thanked him for his help in tracing the renegade soldier. After so many years, the threat to the lives and property of the Pusztai family had finally been ended. Now, Demeter could marry his niece Theresa and perhaps Jack would take his wife and family, with young Paul Pusztai to the wedding. He had already made up his mind that any future foreign travel would only be for showing his family the many beautiful overseas cities and beaches of Europe. He would also now be able to spend most of his time with his family in Liverpool and might even begin working on new ideas to expand his company.